Did you [barcode] ›oks?

CW01590434

TM

This book is for Nick, who made me finish it.
With all my love always.

CHAPTER ONE

'WILL YOU...?'

Lucy Telford leaned forward expectantly, mouth slightly open, sea-green eyes wide. So certain was she of how this sentence would end that for a moment she actually thought she'd heard the words 'marry me'. But by the time her brain caught up and performed a reality check, Ed had moved on to describing the cottage for sale on the outskirts of Bath—on which he hoped she would supply the deposit. And it dawned on her to her utter disbelief: it had happened again.

She drove grimly through the quiet streets of the city early the following morning. Apparently the strength of cliché and female experience on her side meant nothing in the face of the male inability to take a hint. It was Valentine's Day, *check*. She was out with her boyfriend of two years, relationship good, *check.* He'd booked her favourite restaurant, bought her favourite flowers and told her he had something special to ask her that evening. *Check, check, check.* What girl wouldn't have expected a marriage proposal given a situation like that? Add in the heavy hints she'd been dropping for at least the last six months. Surely the odds were somewhere approaching dead cert?

She tightened her grip on the steering wheel, her face set, her dark curls even more defiantly springy than usual, reflecting the way she felt. The rest of the evening had passed in an angry red blur. The night hadn't been much better. She'd tossed and turned, alternately hot and throwing the covers off, then freezing cold. Then somewhere around two a solution of sorts had come to her. A way of taking control.

She pulled the car into a roadside space in one of Bath's lovely streets, the golden stone of the Georgian terrace picked out by the winter sunshine. It was a perfect February morning, icy cold but bright. Running her own bakery business had made her accustomed to extremely early starts and she adored the way the city looked when it was still half asleep. It did nothing to distract her today.

Killing the engine, she stalked, as well as she could in trainers, across the pavement and up the stone steps to the three-storey town house of the one person she could moan at unreservedly. The one person who would let her vent her anger, calm her down and give her an objective opinion on what she should do. Childhood friend, adult protector, confidant and big-brother figure, Gabriel Blake was about to kiss his Sunday morning lie-in goodbye.

Gabriel tried mashing one of the pillows over his head and holding it against both ears but the ringing simply faded to a more annoying level. Opening one eye to glance at the bedside clock, he groaned. Seven-thirty. He only knew one person who got up this early on a Sunday. The ringing continued and he eventually crawled from the bed and staggered half asleep down the stairs, gripping the banister for support. His thick dark hair stood up in crazy sleep spikes and a shadow of stubble defined his strong jaw. He rubbed at his scratchy eyes. By now she had obviously tired of intermittent ringing and was simply keeping the button depressed, resulting in a constant noise that challenged his impending hangover like an ice pick.

He opened the door a crack and, closing his aching eyes against the morning sun, he snarled through the gap. 'Lucy, it's seven-thirty on a Sunday morning. What the hell do you think you're doing?'

'You've got your eyes shut. How did you know it was me?'

'Nobody else I know would dare disturb me at this time of the morning.' He opened one eye and squinted at her. 'Especially on a Sunday.'

She made a move to lean around the front door and see past him into the house, glancing indifferently as she did so at his toned torso and the muscular broad shoulders that were set off by the remains of a tan from his last trip abroad. She'd stayed with him in this house for a while a year or so ago and as a result she had developed a unique immunity to the fact that with no shirt on he looked like a god. Unlike the rest of the female race, to her he just looked like Gabriel. Best friend of some twenty-three years. No romantic attraction involved.

'Is there someone with you?' she asked him

bossily. 'Because if there is, get rid of them. This is an emergency.'

He ran a hand through his hair, mussing it more than ever, and tried to think straight. 'There's no one here—it's just me. What do you mean an emergency? Are you OK?'

'I can't discuss it on the doorstep. Let me in!'

He leaned wearily back against the wall and she lost no time in pushing past him like a tornado into the hall. He looked longingly back up the curving stairway in the direction of his bedroom and waved a mental white flag. Now he'd let her in the house there was no way sleep was going to be on the cards. He closed the front door and followed her resignedly to the kitchen to put coffee on.

She turned as he entered the room and he felt a fresh stab of exasperation as he noticed for the first time she was wearing jogging gear. Three-quarter-length running shorts hugged her lean frame, giving away for once the fact that she was fit and toned. She was so tiny that ordinary loose clothes gave her the impression of fragility. Ironic, he sometimes thought, that someone whose life revolved around cake should be so slender. Her dark curls were caught up in a band, but tendrils escaped as usual around her face. The clothes could only mean one thing. She intended to persuade him to go running with her when he still had at least three hours' sleep to catch up on.

On the brink of losing his already frayed temper, he saw just in the nick of time the dark smudges under her green eyes, starkly contrasting with the creamy complexion, and the troubled expression on her face. Unable to feel anything but protective towards her when she was unhappy ever since she was six years old and he was eight, he abandoned his mission to fill the kettle and gave her a hug instead. He couldn't help noticing the stiffness in the muscles of her shoulders even through her clothes, and her hands against his bare skin as they slid around his waist were cold enough to make him jump. Everything about her exuded tension.

'What's up?' He spoke gently over her head, which nestled perfectly just under his chin, coils of her caught-up hair brushing his jaw lightly. Her hair had a lovely lemony scent, making him dimly aware that he could do with a shower. She didn't seem to notice, though, as she made no move to pull away from his chest, and she would normally be the first person to point out if he smelled of last night's curry. 'Tell me it's something serious to justify waking me up before eleven on a Sunday.'

She looked up at him in obvious anguish.

'Oh, God, it's not one of your parents, is it? Are they ill?'

Now she pulled back to arm's length, an expression of incredulity on her face. 'Something happening to either of my nightmare parents doesn't come very high on the serious metre—you of all people should know that.'

'OK, then,' he conceded. 'It obviously *isn't* to do with your wonderful parents.' He ignored Lucy as she made a face. 'But I'm not up to playing guessing games. Come and sit down and tell me what's up.'

Abandoning the coffee, he pulled her by the hand into the sitting room, shoved aside a pile of newspapers and dragged her down next to him on one of the squashy white sofas. She gazed down at her tiny hands, the nails always short and never varnished because that interfered with her baking.

'It's Ed.' One of her hands crept up to her mouth and she chewed on one of the thumbnails distractedly.

'I knew it! What's the idiot done now?' He had no real opinion of Ed. There seemed nothing about him to provoke strong feelings one way or the other. He seemed to treat Lucy well enough and he didn't interfere with their friendship. That was all Gabriel really cared about. She always seemed too focused on building up her bakery business to be serious about anyone.

'It's not what he's done.' She looked at him miserably. 'It's what he hasn't done.'

'I'm not following.'

She sighed. 'We've been together now for, what, two years. It's all going fine, ticking along, you know.' He nodded encouragingly. 'And at Christmas, I thought that was going to be it…'

'What was going to be it?' His head had begun to ache. He wished she'd get to the point.

'When he gave me the necklace. You know, the moon-shaped silver one?' She searched his face. Gabriel had no idea what she was talking about but nodded anyway. 'He handed the box over with this big grand gesture and I thought for sure that was it. I would open it and there would be the ring.' She held a hand out, palm upturned, as if expecting the non-existent ring to materialise there in front of her eyes.

So this was it.

'You mean you thought he was going to propose and it turned out he'd bought you a necklace?' He laughed, feeling an unexpected flash of passing sympathy for Ed. Women. Sometimes there was no pleasing them. 'Hey, at least he bought you a necklace!'

She threw her hands up in exasperation. 'You're missing the point. What was last night?'

He scratched his head. 'You've got me. Saturday night?'

She shoved him. 'No, you idiot. It was Valentine's Day, wasn't it? Surely you must remember that—the postman probably got a hernia heaving your sackload of cards up the steps.' She looked away and muttered disgustedly almost to herself, 'I can't *believe* you don't remember.'

'Of course, of course, Valentine's Day. I did get a few cards as it happens.' He glanced at the waste-paper bin in the corner, into which he'd dropped all the love-related correspondence of the previous day.

'I don't care about your cards! It was Valentine's Day, and Ed had booked a table at our favourite restaurant, that Italian one, you know. And he'd told me he had something special to discuss with me. And I thought, well…'

Gabriel sighed. He could see where this was heading. 'You thought he was going to propose.'

'Yes.'

'And did he?'

'No! He started going on about this investment opportunity and wondering if I might consider putting some money in. The bakery has been doing pretty well lately…' She trailed off miserably.

Gabriel looked at her, torn between concern for her and amusement. He'd known, of course, that she had a bit of a dream of ending up with the perfect happily ever after. Marriage, two-point-four children and a dog. How could he not know that when they'd been friends for so long? After the insecurities of her childhood it made perfect sense that she would want to build her own secure family in later life. But he'd never seriously considered it would happen in the foreseeable future; she was far too ambitious and engrossed in her growing business. And he'd never for a moment considered Ed as…

As what? Competition? His stomach did a slow and unexpected flip, adding to the hangover symptoms he was gradually developing. Where the hell had that thought come from? *As permanent fixture material,* he corrected himself. He must really need some sleep; he wasn't thinking straight. He put a hand to his head and massaged his temples with his thumb and forefinger. 'Lu, it's just one of those things. He hasn't done this to upset you—he probably hasn't got a clue you feel like this. Did you tell him?'

She shook her head.

'You know what Ed's like. It probably doesn't occur to him that you might like him to propose marriage.' Gabriel didn't particularly consider Ed to be the sharpest knife in the drawer, but, even if he was, mind-reading was likely to be beyond him. 'It doesn't mean he isn't happy, does it?'

She shrugged. He decided to try a more brutal tack. He felt an unexpected compulsion to talk her out of the marriage dream. Nothing to do with disliking Ed. If anything he was completely neutral on that subject. But Lucy was only just approaching thirty. She was far too ambitious to settle down; this would turn out to be one of her temporary crazes. Occasionally she got a mad idea into her head and threw her heart and soul into it, only to tire of it ten minutes later. The only thing she'd ever been totally committed to was creative cookery.

Straight talking was what was needed here. He took a deep breath. 'Look, Lucy, you really need to get over this sudden obsession with settling down, with marriage. Marriage isn't the be-all and end-all of everything these days, you know. Loads of people are happy just dating long term, or maybe moving in together. And don't forget your business has just taken off. Ed probably just thinks there's no rush.' As an afterthought he added, 'And he's right.'

She shook her head vigorously. 'You're not getting it. I know loads of people don't go for marriage these days and that's up to them. But this is about me. And for me moving in together is a cop out. Not enough.'

She looked up at him, her green eyes wide and clear. He felt as if he could see every fleck of colour in them. 'My parents just lived together and one or other of them was always either about to leave, leaving, or left. Maybe if they'd been married they might have taken it all a bit more seriously. Moving in is not enough of a commitment. Not for me. Not deep down.' She made a fist and pressed it against her flat stomach. 'Ed has no excuse. He's more than up for getting married when we discuss it in principle, which we have done *loads* of times.'

Gabriel stood up and started back to the kitchen. He needed coffee and painkillers. Not necessarily in that order. The hangover was kicking in with a vengeance.

She called after him. 'He's quite happy to say of course he wants to get married one day. But when it comes to actually stepping up to the plate and making it official? Nothing! I've had it up to here!' She indicated a level somewhere above her head. 'I obviously attract commitment-phobic men. And so that's why I've come to get your help.'

He stopped in his tracks halfway to the door and looked back at her dubiously. 'What do you mean, *my* help? What the hell can I do?'

'You have loads of girlfriends, right? And you're the most commitment-shy person I know.'

'Well, yes...I mean no.' He tried to work out

if there was a compliment or insult in there and decided there was probably both. 'How is this relevant?'

'Well, I've decided to take matters into my own hands,' she said firmly. 'There's no point hanging around waiting for Ed to get his act together. I'll be ninety before that happens and my clock is ticking.'

Gabriel pulled a revolted face. 'OK, can we not talk about the clock-ticking thing? Men don't want to know about that biological time-bomb stuff. In fact, if you've mentioned that to Ed, it could be your reason right there.'

She held up a hand to shut him up. 'Exactly my point. You can advise me on all this kind of thing.'

He raised his eyebrows at her quizzically.

'Where I'm going wrong, of course. Why he isn't falling over himself to get a ring on my finger.' She warmed to her subject. 'You must have a *wealth* of experience just waiting to be tapped. You can show me how to be totally irresistible to him. And then…' she swept past him into the kitchen and crashing sounds began as she started to make the coffee herself '…I'm going to ask him to marry me. On February twenty-ninth.'

He thought for a moment she might actually be going mad.

'It's a leap year,' she supplied helpfully, as if she had read his mind. 'Women have a chance, no, a *right* to propose to their man on this day, once every four years. And you are going to help me do it in a way which means he will have to say yes!'

Hangover forgotten, he barged into the kitchen behind her. She'd had some crazy ideas in her time, but this…

'No. Absolutely no way.'

'Why not?' She looked up from scrabbling about in the cutlery drawer to give him a petulant frown.

'Because I don't have time to provide you with an insight into the male mind, and, even if I did, it's not right, Lucy. You have to go home, tell Ed how unhappy you are and force the issue.'

'Do you think I haven't tried that?' Her voice began to take on an angry pitch. 'I did all of that at Christmas, he was totally clear on my feelings and gave me the same old rubbish about it "happening one day soon". It's made absolutely zero difference.' She slammed two cups down on the counter so hard he was amazed they didn't break. 'He bought me perfume for my birthday—another missed opportunity right there—and now Valentine's Day. The most romantic day of the year and we spent the evening discussing cash flow for his property development business.'

Gabriel shook a generous mound of instant coffee directly from the jar into his cup. If he was going to survive this conversation he needed all the caffeine he could get. 'Have you considered that maybe he just isn't the right guy?'

Her face twisted and the anger gave way to frustration. 'He *is* the right guy, Gabe. We get on great. He's supportive, he makes me laugh and I love him. He's got his own business like me, so he understands when I disappear on evenings and weekends to finish off wedding cakes…'

None of these things particularly struck Gabriel as evidence of true love—more like plenty of free time to watch football on the weekend and free evenings to go out with his mates.

'Please, Gabe. I'll do the same for you one day.'

'I have absolutely no need of help on how to propose to women, thanks very much.'

'I wasn't suggesting that. I just meant I'd owe you a favour. I know you've denounced commitment since Alison died.' She looked at him uncertainly, and well she might. She knew perfectly well this would touch a nerve.

He felt the usual stab in his chest, where his heart was, he supposed. It was a low blow mentioning Alison. He devoted most of his waking hours to keeping all memory of her locked in a corner of his mind that he never visited. He certainly had no intention of talking about her now. He fixed a neutral expression on his face and grappled for a subject change. Thinking on his feet being one of his strengths, he very quickly found one.

'Now that you mention owing me a favour...' He spun away from her suddenly and grabbed a gilt-edged piece of stiff cream card from beneath a magnet on the fridge. 'Will you come to my law firm dinner with me?' He passed her the card and she scrutinised it.

'You want me to be your date for some work do?' she asked. 'I thought you had them queuing up? Can't that Tabitha go with you? Or is it Agatha? God, I lose track.'

'Tabitha was months ago, keep up. I think you must mean Susan.'

'Who the hell is Susan?'

'It doesn't matter, to be honest. We broke up last week. She was getting a bit full-on.' Unable to find a clean teaspoon in his bombsite of a kitchen, he began to stir his coffee with a fork handle.

'Well, in that case, you should be due to meet someone new…' she consulted her watch with a flourish '…any time right about now. The dinner's in a couple of weeks, so she should be at the perfect point in your relationship. Falling for you, but not yet far enough to scare you into dropping her like a hot potato. Problem solved—you really don't need me. And anyway…' she passed the invitation back to him and picked up her cup '…we're talking about *my* problem, not your logistical dating rubbish.'

He shook his head. 'You don't understand. This is serious. I can't be taking just anyone. It's a big deal, this dinner, all our major clients will be there, and all the partners in the firm. I need a date who isn't too showy and who won't be draped all over me or hanging on my every word. In short, someone who will act the way I ask them to. That's where you come in.

Tabitha will be there, too, since she works for us, and things didn't really end well with her.'

She raised her eyebrows. 'Are you for real? You're so arrogant. Have you ever thought it might be the type of woman you go for that causes the problem? Or maybe, shock-horror, the way you treat them? You never show any interest beyond a couple of dates.'

He shrugged. 'I'm always honest with them. I never give the impression that I want anything serious. It's not normally an issue, but the thing is I've dated a couple of the women at work, women who'll be at the dance. You're well known as just a friend of mine. So no chance of any jealous scenes. No one will feel remotely threatened by you. Problem solved.'

Lucy gave a cynical laugh. 'I wouldn't be convinced of that. Your girlfriends are never my biggest fans. Women are eternally suspicious of the female best friend. You automatically wonder what he's getting from her that he can't get from you.'

Gabriel was mystified. 'No, no. They always say they like you. And they know you're with Ed.'

'They would say that. They're trying to please you. You really could do with my insight, you know.' She sighed. 'But look, I'll make a bargain with you. I will go to the dinner with you and solve your dating problems.'

He grinned triumphantly, but she held up a hand. 'Please, let me finish. On condition that you help me with my proposal plan. I need the male point of view.' She looked at him expectantly. 'Do we have a deal? I thought we could start right away. We could go for a run by the river and discuss some details.' She stood up and did a couple of sample stretches, lunging forward on her slightly built legs.

He watched her in horrified amazement. 'You're insane if you think I'm up to running anywhere. I only got to bed at three.'

Was it just that? He felt an irrational negativity towards the idea of helping her propose to Ed, and crushed it. It must be the hangover. Why should he care if she got married, as long as she was happy? That was all he ever wanted for her, after all. Based on past experience she would be bored with the idea in a couple of weeks, and if he got her to look closely enough at Ed's faults he might even be able to speed it up and everything would get back to normal. Best to just go with the flow for now.

'Let me go back to bed and I'll come round

to your place tomorrow night,' he said. 'I'll even bring a bottle of wine. And, though I say it with a measure of dread, *then* you've got a deal.'

CHAPTER TWO

DESPITE Gabriel's protestations that he needed sleep, after Lucy left to go running and he fell gratefully back into bed it totally eluded him. *Lucy getting married.* His mind worried at it like a dog at a bone. It was a given that if she were to propose, Ed would accept. He didn't question that for a second. Any man would be a fool to refuse her. Knowing her as he did, she would storm ahead with the arrangements and be married by the end of the year. Her life would revolve around someone else then. His mind picked at this one thing. Where was the space for their friendship in that?

When she wanted help with anything Gabriel was the one she came to. It had been the same since they were kids. Hell, it had been him who'd found the property that was now her first shop, and persuaded her to move to Bath and expand her successful cake business, which up until then had operated through word of mouth from her own kitchen. He'd even let her live with him rent free for six months while she got the shop off the ground. If something really great or really bad happened to him she was the first person he wanted to tell about it. The great things because he knew she'd get a kick out of them just as he did. The bad things because her effervescent personality always made him feel better, no matter what kind of day he'd had. How did he feel about having someone else step into that role? If he were totally, brutally honest he hated the thought. Sleep was a long time coming.

Three hours later, Lucy was peeling potatoes in her cosy little kitchen when the front door slammed and Ed came into the flat. He gave her a smacking kiss and looked over her shoulder at the pans of vegetables.

'Hi, baby. Smells great.'

'Thanks.'

He was wearing a T-shirt and tracksuit bottoms, hair still slightly damp from the shower. Ed played for a local football team and trained most Sunday mornings. He opened the fridge and took out two beers, holding one out to her. She shook her head.

'No, thanks, I'm fine. How was training?' She didn't mind him playing. It was the one day of the week when she had a relaxed morning to herself. Except for this morning, of course. She felt exasperated still with Ed's insensitivity the night before, but she was doing something about it now, wasn't she? In a couple of weeks' time they would be engaged. She smiled inwardly at the thought.

'OK. Knee's been giving me a bit of grief. Think I'll go and put it up for a bit. Anything I can do?'

'No, no. You go and sit down. I'll just get the potatoes on and then I'll be in.'

When she entered the lounge ten minutes later Ed was sprawled in the armchair, sports channel on the TV, foot resting on the coffee table.

She sat down on the arm of his chair and ruffled his blond hair affectionately. It fell over his forehead and the sideburns were grown long in homage to Ed's music hero Elvis Presley. 'I saw Gabriel this morning. I was going to drag him out jogging but he was hung way over. In the end I went on my own.'

'Hmm.' He didn't avert his gaze from the TV screen.

'He's asked me if I'll go to a dinner dance thing with him. It's a work do.'

Ed glanced up at her.

'Can't he take one of his women? God knows there's enough of them.'

She smiled. 'That's exactly what I said. Apparently he's offended one of his ex-girlfriends and she's going to be there. He needs a neutral date to avoid any grief. It's the weekend after next—you don't mind, do you?'

He took a swig from the bottle of beer. 'No. I'll go out with the lads probably. You go and enjoy yourself. Keep him in check.'

'He's coming round tomorrow night, too. Got a few work issues to discuss, but you'll be out anyway.'

He simply nodded, clearly more attuned to the television than to her. She watched him. There had been a time, once, when they'd first got together, that they would have had a stand-up row at her suggestion she have a night out with Gabriel. The few boyfriends she'd had before Ed had been the same. She didn't blame them. It normally took a good few months before they realised her relationship with Gabriel really was totally platonic and then they quit protesting and questioning her about him. Even so, Ed still couldn't resist the occasional dig, and liked to amuse himself by promoting the view that Gabe took advantage of her friendship when it suited him. But he didn't try to stop her seeing him, and that was all that really mattered to her. She simply rose above the masculine posturing.

After lunch, she watched Ed as he stacked dishes in the dishwasher. This was exactly what she liked so much about being with him. Domesticity. Her mind wandered before she could stop it towards her own childhood home. She had lived with her parents in the tied cottage on Gabriel's family estate. The cottage went with her father's job of groundsman. Anything to do with the upkeep of the manor house and its gardens and outhouses had been his responsibility. And to his credit, she thought, he did a good job for almost the entire time they were there. Until the end when his drinking had more charge of his life than he did himself.

Dragged down with him was her mother, who developed her own drinking problem alongside him, almost in sympathy with him.

The rows had become more and more frequent, verbal at first, then at times physical. By the time Lucy was sixteen her mother had left and she was running the house herself as well as managing her own schoolwork. She had kept everything perfectly as if she could somehow bring order to the rest of her life by making the house run smoothly.

Watching Ed now in her tiny kitchen, helping her clear up after eating the meal she had cooked for them both, she felt a warmth deep inside her. She felt totally at ease, relaxed, secure. She wanted that feeling to last and to envelop every aspect of her life. She wanted to start thinking about having children now, a family of her own to look after. It was the logical next step for them, and getting married was the way she wanted to start that journey. She felt excited at the thought of it—a proper family at last.

The following evening, Gabriel was late as usual. *Only in his private life, though,* Lucy thought fondly as she tidied up. He was always impeccably presented, perfectly prepared and absolutely on time when he was working. In fact he was the most professional person she knew, totally reliable and with absolute integrity when he had his lawyer hat on. A rising star in legal circles, he had attained partnership before the age of thirty and his career was going from strength to strength. Unfortunately it never seemed to wrap over to his personal life. He was always late and his beautiful house was always a pigsty.

She let him in and he kissed her on the cheek. She caught a whiff of his aftershave, something woody that made her want to breathe in deeply. He marched straight through into her neat little kitchen, grabbed a couple of glasses and rummaged in the drawer for a bottle opener. She followed him in and leaned against the doorway, watching him with amused interest.

'Make yourself at home,' she said teasingly.

He grinned without looking up. 'You're such a creature of habit, Lu. After living with you for six months I could probably find any given kitchen utensil or crockery item in this room without even looking.'

'Steak knife?'

He opened the drawer below the hob and pulled the knife out with a flourish. She liked all sharp items to be close to hob and chopping board.

'Luck!' she protested. 'Olive oil?'

He pointed at the high cupboard on the left. 'In the ingredients and condiments cupboard, of course.'

She didn't have to open the cupboard to know he was right. Everything in her kitchen had order to it. She liked it that way. 'Salad spinner?'

'What the hell is one of those?'

She laughed and he grinned back at her as he uncorked the bottle of wine.

'OK, let's get started.' She took one of the glasses and led the way into her little sitting room. It was neat and tidy. The scented candles she'd lit earlier gave off a delicious warm winter scent of orange and cloves. He followed with the bottle and took the armchair. She settled herself close by on the sofa.

'So, where do you think we should start, then?' she asked him as soon as she was comfortable.

He glanced up at her as he poured the wine.

'Should I ask him on his own, or with all our friends and family there?' She put her head on one side and screwed her nose up, considering. 'Do you think it would be too weird if I bought myself a ring?'

He held up a hand for her to be quiet and she waited impatiently while he took a slug from his glass. 'Firstly, for the record, I want you to know I think this is possibly the most crackpot idea you've ever had. I'm including in that the time when we were kids and you convinced me my mother would be pleased if we repainted the sitting-room door yellow with my fingerpaints.'

She laughed and he smiled back at her. He had a heart-melting smile that gradually crept up to his eyes, creasing the corners and giving him a look of intensity. She always felt he kept that smile just for her. No doubt many other women felt the same, she thought wryly.

'But since you've agreed to watch my back at this wretched work dinner dance,' he went on, 'I will help you.'

She clapped her hands together excitedly.

'But if we do this, we're going to take it seriously and we're going to do it my way. OK?' He looked at her sternly for agreement.

'OK.' She sat on her hands to keep herself from fidgeting, and made herself wait for him to carry on. Once Gabriel had committed to something she knew he would take it totally seriously and wouldn't allow her to sidetrack him with her enthusiasm. It was one of the things she adored about him.

In all the years she'd known him, he'd never let her down. Unlike most of the other main players in her life, she thought, with a pang of regret. The finger-painting memory reminded her of how much she'd loved spending time with him as a child. Gabriel was an only child, just like her, except that his parents were very loving and very wealthy. She hadn't cared about the wealthy part, but she had envied him for the happy, unworried and loving life he had. His family were warm and kind and had always welcomed her. For her the 'big house', as she'd thought of it, had been a refuge from the constant escalating fights in her own home.

Gabriel dragged her back to the present by making an enthusiastic start on his plans. 'OK, there's only two weeks until the twenty-ninth so we need to get our skates on. That means radical plans to make him sit up and take notice of you.' He leaned back a little and looked at her critically. 'I know you, Lucy. You'll be wanting to jump in and plan a massive party culminating with you getting down on one knee. But it's not enough to plan a speech and a big sweeping gesture of a proposal.' He paused for effect. 'For true success you need to get to the bottom of why he doesn't feel he needs to propose to you himself. If we can do that we can change the way he thinks of you and we'll be guaranteed a positive outcome.' He grinned at her across the coffee table.

'How do we do that?' She marvelled at how well he knew her. It was almost spooky. One of the options she'd been secretly considering was a party ending in a firework display. Another was hiring a barbershop quartet to sing the proposal to Ed while she looked smugly on awaiting his resounding 'yes'. Her own enthusiasm could easily overshadow her common sense, which was why Gabriel's calm perspective was exactly what was needed.

'We're going to scrutinise every area of your life,' he said. 'Find out why he needs a rocket lit under him to get him to commit. We'll look at your home life, your social life, your wardrobe, your appearance...' He sat back again for a moment and looked her up and down appraisingly from the extra distance. His slate-grey eyes looked puffy and sleep-starved, but nothing could detract from the strong jawline and determined mouth. *Even when he's tired he looks gorgeous,* she thought. *How unfair. And now he's going to criticise the way I look.*

She pushed her fingers through her curls defensively. 'What's the matter with my appearance?' she demanded.

He leaned forward again to pick up his glass. 'Nothing, sweetie, except that Ed is used to you looking like that. We need to make him see you through fresh eyes and the easiest way to do that is by working on your appearance. I know someone who runs the personal shopping service at Jolly's in town. Leave it to me.'

'Right,' she said dubiously. 'Because if your intention is to boost my ego, let me tell you you're falling way short.'

He ignored her. 'Tell me about your average day.'

'Weekday or weekend?' His businesslike attitude was beginning to tug at the edges of her temper. This was her life they were talking about after all, not some legal transaction.

'Weekday. What do you both do? When do you see each other? How often do you get together?'

'Wow, twenty questions.'

He simply looked at her expectantly, eyebrows raised as if she were a misbehaving toddler, and she spoke quickly before he could admonish her for not taking it seriously. 'Well, I get up early, of course. Usually about five so I can get to the bakery and sort out the stock for the day. So he rarely stays over on a weeknight.'

'So you don't see him during the week except in the evening?'

'Well, no, but he usually rings me every day mid-morning,' she said brightly. 'That's if he's not in the middle of something at one of the houses.'

Ed was a property developer. Fed up with his job in IT, he'd given it all up three years ago, just before they'd met in fact, and now spent his time buying run-down shacks and doing them up, then selling them on for profit. It wasn't yet turning out to be the giant money-spinner he always talked it up to be.

Still, early days, she told herself. Give the guy a chance. She liked the fact that he'd thrown himself into building up a business, being his own boss. Taking responsibility for his own success or failure. It was something she could relate to. After all, it had taken her years of hard graft to build up her cake business. They had a lot in common, and that always made for a good, strong relationship, in her opinion.

Gabriel pressed on. 'And how much does he actually do around the house?'

'Plenty.'

'Not good enough. What's his house like? Imagine you're married and living together in this lovely flat.'

She glanced around the perfectly tidy room with satisfaction. She loved her little flat, filled with unusual bits and pieces of furniture that she'd picked up in markets and antique shops. Gabriel had always teased her about it, telling her she was 'nesting'.

'Imagine you go away on holiday or business for a week,' he went on. 'You leave him alone here. Based on what you know of him, what would the place be like when you got back?'

She pulled a face. 'Well, he's not that good on his own, to be honest. He's not really a cook, so he'd probably have lived on pizza and takeaways. The place would most likely look just like his house. A hovel. You'd feel at home in it!' She dodged as he threw a cushion at her.

'I'm not that bad!'

'Your flat is a pigsty, Gabe. Face facts. The only time there's been any semblance of order was when I stayed with you and that's only because I can't live in your kind of squalor.'

'You're not doing yourself any favours here, you know.' He put on a hurt expression. 'Anyway, we're talking about Ed, not me. What else?'

She pursed her mouth, considering. 'There'd be an overload of washing. I'm not sure he knows how to work the machine.'

'Pathetic!'

'And the plants would probably be dead. He never remembers to water them.'

He held up a hand to stop her. 'I think I've heard enough. Basically, Lu, and I'm going to be brutal here…' She looked at him expectantly. He paused dramatically then announced loudly, 'You have become Ed's mother.'

Silence for a moment while this sank in and then she exploded. 'Don't be so ridiculous! You're twisting everything. You make it sound like he's some layabout slob who doesn't lift a finger while I do everything!'

'Sounds about right.'

She stood up, feeling irrationally that it

might somehow give her the advantage to be taller than him. 'You're wrong, Gabriel. We're just very different people with different priorities. There must be millions, zillions of couples just like us.'

'I'm sure there are,' he said with calm amusement. 'But what you *think* you have is the traditional "he hunts it, she cooks it" model of relationship. Only trouble is, unless he changes his ways *you* will hunt it *and* cook it because, face it, if you get married to Ed, you are going to be the main breadwinner.'

'That has nothing to do with it!'

'It has everything to do with it!'

Hands on hips, she glared at him angrily.

He held his hands up in a calm-down gesture. 'OK, let's take a different approach. Have you told him about going to the dinner as my date yet?'

'Yes,' she said, relaxing a little at the change of tack. She sat down again. Ed had been more than reasonable when she'd asked him. *Let's see you pick holes in that, Gabriel.*

'And what did he say?'

'He was totally fine about it, as a matter of fact. Didn't bat an eyelid. Even told me to have a good time,' she said triumphantly.

'Oh, dear.' He looked at her sympathetically. 'What now?'

'Well, it's good for me, of course, problem solved for the dinner and dance. But for you… you are being taken for granted! Big time.'

She felt her temper strain madly at its leash. This was rapidly becoming a character assassination of Ed and she wasn't going to take it lying down. 'I don't see that,' she countered coldly. 'Surely it's a positive thing that he's being so reasonable.'

'Aha! That's where you're wrong.' He leaned in close to her suddenly, grabbed her wrist and looked into her eyes. Her stomach made a sudden unexpected flutter and she felt her pulse increase. She ignored it, assuming it must be part of the effort required to keep her temper from flaring. 'Lucy, if I was in a relationship with you, lovely you, I would not let you go on a date with any other guy but me. I wouldn't care whether he was your friend, if he was gay, whatever.'

She looked into his eyes. Clear slate grey filled with nothing but genuine love and concern for her. The pit of her stomach felt warm and soft suddenly, like melting chocolate. She felt the tiny spark of a long-forgotten memory, almost there and then gone again. Her mind felt adrift, as if sand had suddenly shifted below her and she was no longer standing firm. *What the hell is this?* Grappling for self-control, she focused hard on her train of thought.

'He used to be like that when we first met,' she protested in a small voice. 'He couldn't stand the sight of you.'

'There you go.' He released her hand and sat back with a triumphant nod, grabbing his wine glass as he went. She felt an odd sensation of loss and put her hand in her lap to compensate. 'He's got used to the fact that you will always be here, you'll never look at anyone else, no one else will ever look at you…'

'Hey!'

'I'm not criticising you, Lu, I'm just telling you that he's got complacent. He's taking you for granted. No need to make an effort because he counts on you always being here. Stopped working at it, hasn't he? That's the key.' He was nodding his head emphatically.

'What is?' She was rapidly losing the point of this conversation. Hadn't it been to focus on the positives of her relationship? Instead he seemed to be implying that Ed was coasting along and taking her for granted. Just what was going on here?

'He thinks he's got it all sewn up. He doesn't need to propose to you because he's already got you. What we need to do is shake that perception up a bit. Make the ground shake a little bit underneath him. Make him realise how fabulous and gorgeous you are and that he has to work to keep you.'

That sounded a bit more like it. 'OK, so how do we do that, Sherlock?'

'You need to move the goalposts,' he said firmly. 'One of the things you can do is see a bit more of me. Get him to miss you a bit. I'm the winner then, too, because I get to spend a bit more time with you. I've missed you since you moved out.'

The warmth in her stomach bubbled back up again and she took a hefty slug of wine to stop it. That strange sense pervaded her again, of falling backwards in time. She shook her head as if to clear it. Of course, she assured herself firmly, it was perfectly normal to feel nervous and emotional. She was sitting here planning her future, after all.

'Have you?' She'd missed him at first, too, after she'd moved out of his house. It had been lovely seeing him every day for those few months after her arrival in Bath.

'Yes.' He grinned mischievously. 'The house has a more relaxed look about it without your obsessive tidying and I get to keep the remote control to myself. But I kind of miss having a fridge full of proper food and coming home to someone. I liked talking to you every day.'

She took another glug of wine and reminded herself that this was Gabe she was talking to. Her best friend with her best interests at heart. He wouldn't be trying to assassinate her relationship; he really was only trying to help, which, after all, was what she'd asked him to do. 'Aww, that's sweet. Bit of a backhanded compliment though. And "relaxed" isn't a word I'd use to describe your hovel. You've got a nerve criticising Ed's domesticity.'

'This isn't about me, though, is it? And anyway, backhanded compliments are the best kind. I'm saying I wish you still lived with me despite all your faults. Not the same as wanting you to change.'

'Hmm, I suppose so,' she said grudgingly.

He refilled her glass, then his own. 'So you agree on how to proceed? Excellent. Why don't you come to lunch with my parents this Sunday? They'd love to see you. They're always asking about you.'

'You mean go back to Gloucestershire?' She felt a vague sense of unease and squashed it. She generally avoided going back to her home county, as if the new life she'd built since leaving would somehow be challenged by revisiting her old one. Her parents were long gone from there, of course, but the memories wouldn't be.

'Of course. Sunday roast. Not cooked by you. Sound tempting?' He grinned at her expectantly.

She debated to herself. She knew she should put an end to the avoidance of anything relating to her childhood. She was an adult now and could recognise it for what it was. Maybe going back to Gloucestershire would do her good—she could lay a few ghosts, and she had to admit he had a point about Ed. Wasn't absence meant to make the heart grow fonder? They had fallen into a bit of a rut recently, doing the same things on the same days.

She gave in. 'It does sound tempting. And I suppose you could be right—perhaps Ed needs to miss me a bit.'

'He definitely does. He needs to appreciate you a bit more and feel like he's lucky to have you and he ought to snap you up officially just to make sure. He feels too sure of you, that's the root of the whole thing. And in the meantime, we'll have a look at your appearance and see what we can do with that. And I need to observe you out together socially.'

Lucy looked doubtfully down at her plain T-shirt and jeans with a vague but undeniable feeling of dread at the idea of Gabriel analysing her wardrobe. In an attempt to divert him she latched onto his second suggestion. 'No problem. We're all meeting up tomorrow night at that new wine bar on George Street. You could come along if you like. Do all the observing you want to.'

'Who's we?'

'Ed's friends,' she said. 'Well, mine, too, of course. There's Digger and Yabba, and their other halves, Suzy and Kate. Probably one or two others—it varies depending on who's free.'

'Digger and Yabba,' Gabriel repeated. 'They sound like rejects from some kids' TV show.'

Lucy laughed. 'That's their nicknames. No one in Ed's friendship group is called by their proper name. It's a man thing. Even Ed isn't his real name.'

'You're kidding,' Gabriel said with sudden interest. 'What is his real name?'

'Roland,' she said, expertly ignoring Gabriel as he almost choked on his wine with a sudden snort of laughter. 'Ed is some schoolboy name to do with heading a football or something. I've never questioned it because frankly Roland is awful and Ed suits him far better.'

Gabriel shook his head in mock wonder. 'There's a whole laddish culture going on that seems to have passed me by.'

'You haven't missed much,' she said. 'It might have been vaguely funny once when they were in their teens but there's something a bit sad about having the nickname Yabba when you're pushing thirty and working as a fireman.'

She leaned back on the sofa and looked at him expectantly. 'So what do you think, then?' she asked. 'Do you want to drop in and join us for a drink?'

'Sure,' he said. 'Should be interesting. Are there any single women going?'

She threw her hands up in exasperation. 'For heaven's sake, Gabriel, can't you forget about your next conquest just for one night? Is it too much to ask? You're meant to be concentrating on me and Ed, not chatting up the nearest single woman.'

'I know, I know.' A pause. 'But are there? Any single women going?'

She sighed wearily. 'Well, there's Joanna, I suppose. She's Kate's sister. She's been single for a bit and she's started hanging out with us. But she's been through a horrible break up and the last thing she needs is a three-week dalliance with the likes of you!'

'That hurt!' he protested. 'I just meant it would be nice if I wasn't the only single person there, that's all.'

'Hmm,' she said dubiously. 'I'll believe you. Thousands wouldn't. I take it that means you're coming, then? Eight o'clock at Hardings. I'd tell you not to be late but there would be no point, would there?'

CHAPTER THREE

LUCY glanced at her watch for the third time. Quarter to nine now and still no sign of Gabriel. His habitual lateness never usually bothered her and she was annoyed with herself for letting it get to her this evening. Despite the fact that she'd asked him for help, his negative comments about her relationship with Ed had been getting on her nerves. She'd been looking forward to proving him wrong by showing just how great a time she and Ed had together. Not that tonight seemed to be going that way so far, she admitted to herself. Ed's day hadn't gone well—a structural problem had been picked up at the house he was currently working on and it was going to be costly to have it sorted out. She noticed he'd moved on to whisky from his usual beer and it wasn't even nine yet. Great. Maybe it would be for the best if Gabe didn't turn up after all. The last thing she needed was him to see Ed slowly getting drunk at the opposite end of the table from her. Just how the hell would *that* look?

As if he had somehow read her mind, the door suddenly swung open at the end of the bar and Gabriel sauntered in, absently looking at his mobile phone as he walked, in no rush whatsoever. He glanced up, quickly searched the room and, seeing her, made his way over to their table. She saw out of the corner of her eye Joanna, the only single girl there, sit up imperceptibly as he approached and viewed him herself for a moment with objectivity. He was wearing a dark shirt, open at the neck, quite snug-fitting, which showed off the heavily muscled shoulders and brought out the depth in his grey eyes. Outside the weather was cold with a tinge of fog in the air and the moisture had tousled his dark hair a little. She gave herself a little shake to clear her head and pasted a smile on her face as she got quickly to her feet.

'You came,' she said through slightly gritted teeth. 'Finally.'

'Am I late?' he whispered in her ear as he leaned in to kiss her cheek, and his breath felt warm against her neck. She felt the shivery sensation of goosebumps beginning and moved away from him as quickly as she could.

'No more than usual,' she said, and mustered a more genuine smile before turning to the table. 'Everybody, this is my friend Gabriel. Gabriel, this is Digger and Kate, and Yabba and Suzy. Digger and Yabba play football with Ed.' Nods were exchanged around the table. 'And this is Joanna.' Lucy gestured towards the blonde at the end of the table, who was apparently unable to tear her gaze away from Gabriel. 'And you know Ed, of course.' Ed raised his whisky glass in a perfunctory hello gesture from the other end of the table.

She sat down as Gabriel hooked a spare chair from a nearby table. Fully expecting him to sit next to her, she felt a little piqued as he dragged it two spaces away and sat down between Joanna and Yabba. She was left to continue the conversation with Kate, who was sitting on her left, about the plans she was making for the summer holidays later in the year.

Gabriel lost no time in buying a round of drinks and then quickly immersed himself in quiet conversation with Joanna. Ed was steadily getting drunker at the other end of the table and Lucy sipped her own glass of orange juice defiantly. If this was the way the evening was going to go, with her boyfriend and her best friend both apparently having no need of her to have a good time, she would damn well make the most of her own company.

Time and again her eyes strayed to Gabriel. She found she was able to largely tune out the ongoing conversation with Kate and Suzy, who were planning a shopping trip in the next few weeks, and who invited her along with no real conviction because they were both fully aware that Saturdays were one of the busiest days of the week for the cake shop. The occasional yes or no seemed to maintain her part in the discussion perfectly well. Joanna's curtain of blonde hair swung glossily as she leaned in towards Gabriel. She seemed oblivious to the rest of the table. Lucy felt a stab of annoyance. And she had every right to feel annoyed, she told herself. She'd invited him out after all, to watch her interact with Ed, and yet he'd barely glanced her way even once. Lucy found she was able to make out the occasional snatch of conversation between them.

'…go out for dinner some time…nothing heavy, just a relaxing evening…' she heard Gabriel saying. She picked up her orange juice, trying to keep the smug smile from her face. Same old Gabriel. Get the caveat in up front. No chance of the relationship being any more than a couple of dates, so make it clear from the outset. She noticed the firm set of his jaw at this angle and the way his dark hair curled a little over his collar. He was truly gorgeous. No wonder Joanna was mesmerised. And he certainly seemed to have the gift of making her feel as if she was the only woman in the room for him. Because it didn't appear to matter how often Lucy glanced his way, she might as well have been invisible for all the notice he took of her. She stood up and went to the bar to get another drink, deliberately ignoring them as she passed. Why should she care if Gabriel chatted up yet another woman? It wasn't as if it were anything she hadn't seen before, after all. She picked up the menu at the bar and looked through the fat-laden snack list. If this was going to be a long and extremely dull evening, she'd need something to get her through.

Lucy checked her watch. Six forty-five. They'd only been jogging for five minutes and already she was flagging. She'd had hardly any sleep, tossing and turning half the night, unable to switch off. When she'd eventually dropped off at about three it had felt as if her alarm had gone off ten minutes later. Her head ached horribly. Gabriel seemed as fresh as a daisy however, despite the fact it was so early in the morning. She wondered if he'd be seeing Joanna again and mentally slapped herself down. It was nothing to do with her and she absolutely didn't care.

'So what conclusions did you get from last night, Relationship Guru?' she panted, more to bring her mind back on task than because she really wanted to speak.

Gabriel glanced sideways at her and then slowed to a stop. There was a bench a short way off and he slowed her down too by grabbing her arm, then pointed at the bench as they approached it. 'Let's sit down for a bit, shall we? You look beat.'

She was too out of breath to argue, and frankly the idea of sitting down for a few minutes sounded wonderful. She followed him to the bench and they sat down and gazed out across the still river. The early morning was fresh and cold and she could see her breath, the clouds from her mouth diminishing slowly as her breathing recovered from the run. Gabriel opened a bottle of water and handed it to her.

'It was an interesting evening,' he began.

'I'm surprised you noticed anything that went on between Ed and me,' she grumbled. 'You spent the entire time trying to prise Joanna's phone number out of her.'

'Just setting up my cover,' he protested with a grin. 'Don't want Ed to work out there's something going on, do you? Don't you think he would have wondered what the hell was going on if I'd spent the entire evening watching the two of you interact? Not that you really did,' he added pointedly.

'Hmm,' she said, unconvinced. 'What are your conclusions, then? Tell me there was a point to it all.'

'Of course there was a point to it. I spent a couple of very useful hours observing you and Ed, and what I saw confirmed what I already thought.'

'Which was…?'

'The reason it doesn't occur to Ed to propose to you is because it won't give him anything more than he already has. Except perhaps a large bill for wedding costs.'

Lucy groaned. 'Frankly I was expecting something a bit more insightful than that.'

'I can give you insights. That was just the concise version.' He took a swig from his bottle of water and glanced at his watch.

'Go on, then.'

'OK…' He stood back up and began stretching to keep warm. Lucy made no move to join him. The way her muscles felt this morning a few stretches were going to make no difference. She might as well give up right now and walk home. But not before she'd heard him out.

'First of all, just look at the people you are hanging out with,' he said.

She frowned. 'What about them? I didn't see you moaning last night when you were chatting to Joanna over drinks and nibbles.'

He shook his head at her. 'You're missing the point. They're all settled, aren't they? Well, except for Joanna, but just from a quick conversation with her I can tell she wants to be settled, too. They're all married or about to be married.'

'I see where you're going with this, but you're wrong. Digger and Kate aren't married, they live together—'

'That's only while Kate pushes Digger towards marriage. You can see the pattern with them—it's the same as you and Ed. The only difference is that Digger has actually moved in with her while Ed's hanging on for dear life to his bachelor pad. What I'm trying to say is that marriage is essentially a girl thing. Your average guy has no real drive to get tied down like that. He's quite happy to live with his girl without all the trappings.'

'Marriage isn't just about trappings,' she protested. 'It's a commitment. It gives proper, constant stability.'

'Only if you choose to see it that way,' he countered. 'Living together is a commitment, too, you know. You just don't have to spend a fortune on a wedding in order to do it. But that doesn't make it any less significant.'

She shook her head to try and clear it. He always did this—confused the issue so she ended up questioning her own certainties. 'Get to the point!' she snapped.

He took a deep breath, the way he always did when he was going to say something that he knew would provoke her. 'Part of the reason for you wanting to get married is a subconscious desire to fit in with your social group. And Ed will never ask you unless he's painted into a corner, because when you pare it right down, he has nothing to gain over and above what he's already getting from you. He has the freedom to keep his own social life; he has you looking after him from every angle. And the pair of you already fit in with all his mates. Why go and spend a fortune making it official? Eventually he probably thinks he'll ask you to move in with him, but, hey, there's no rush.'

His sideway glance to measure her reaction told her he knew perfectly well that he was making her angry. Her head ached and her brain felt as if it were swathed in cotton wool. She didn't have the energy to explode at him as she normally would. Instead she settled for sharpening her tone.

'To be perfectly honest, Gabe, this amateur psychology rubbish is starting to get on my nerves. All I want is a few pointers. I don't want or need my whole life deconstructed.' She stood up, wincing at the throb in her head at the sudden movement. 'I'm starting to wish I'd never told you about any of this.'

He shrugged. 'No problem, Lu. I thought you wanted my help, and I'm not going to just tell you stuff you want to hear. That's not how I work. I'll give you my opinion and then it's up to you how you act on it. But what I'm saying is, if you change nothing about your relationship, if you carry on playing the part of a wife before you actually *are* one, then don't expect Ed to propose to you any time soon.'

'I don't expect him to propose any time soon. I'm going to propose to him. Isn't that the whole point of this?'

'Of course. But don't you think it makes sense to work out why he hasn't taken the bull by the horns himself? Then you can make changes that keep him on his toes and stop him taking you for granted. You have to admit that would be a good thing for your relationship. He doesn't seem to feel like he has to make any effort with you at the moment, does he? I mean, just look at him last night, sulking into his whisky glass at the end of the table. I'd be surprised if he said more than ten sentences to you all night. Why does he think it's OK to treat you like that? He might have had a bad day, but that's no excuse. I'll tell you why—it's because you let him think it's OK.'

She looked at his serious expression. The problem with her friendship with Gabriel was that their usual sparring was self-perpetuating. She heard herself talk to him sometimes and thought she really was just arguing for argument's sake because she never wanted to be the one that gave in. She couldn't fail to see that he had a point and she would be an idiot not to accept it. Too tired to keep bickering, she sighed. 'OK, OK, I'll admit I can see where you're coming from.'

To his credit Gabriel obviously knew her well enough to restrain himself from making any gesture or sound of triumph, simply nodding in agreement, and so she felt able to continue calmly rather than taking the plunge back into the row that any crowing on his part would have provoked. 'Where do we go from here, then?' she asked. 'I'm putting myself in your hands.'

He began jogging lightly on the spot. 'Well, the next logical step is your appearance, of course. We've covered your social life, we've looked at the way you react and respond around Ed. Now, you need to make him sit up and take notice. We start with how you look and then we move on to the way you behave. Right?'

'Right,' she repeated, with more conviction than she felt.

'Good,' he said in a businesslike tone. 'Then as you're obviously desperate to quit running you can go home now. Meet me on Thursday night in the city centre.'

Her heart sank.

Lucy locked the door of the cake shop behind her and listened until the alarm system finished beeping and set itself before heading to her battered yellow Mini car. It was already dark outside and she cursed the car's next-to-useless heater, which roasted her right foot but left the rest of her freezing cold as she made her way through the steady traffic into the main city centre. Towards the shops. The knot in her stomach wouldn't go away. She didn't like clothes shopping and applauded the ascent of the Internet, where she could buy what she wanted online in the comfort of her own sitting room, a cup of coffee to hand, and send back anything she didn't like. She had aspirations to extend her cake business one day to encompass online shopping.

Sighing to herself as she parked, she realised that if she wanted to keep expanding her business then the cash investment that seemed so important to Ed wasn't likely to be a reality any time soon. Still, Ed would understand that, she was sure. He was as steady as a rock, one of the things that attracted her to him. Not unpredictable or headstrong. *Not like Gabriel at all,* she thought unexpectedly, and frowned. She had no place thinking that, she admonished herself. It was of no consequence to her how Gabriel differed from Ed; she wasn't one of his endless stream of girlfriends, thank goodness. She had no idea how they put up with him, not knowing if he would be there for the next date or not. She easily silenced the small voice at the back of her mind that protested that unpredictable was a million times more interesting and exciting than steady. It was also a million times less safe.

It was Thursday night, late-night shopping in Bath, and Gabriel had 'called in a favour', as he described it, and organised a personal shopping session for Lucy. Not necessarily to buy anything, he had placated her when she'd raised a frugal eyebrow—Gabriel had expensive tastes and she really didn't need that kind of encouragement. But to try on a few new things and look at the kind of thing men apparently liked their women to wear. According to Gabriel this was a world apart from what women *thought* men liked them to wear.

'A subtle distinction, but by the end of today

I think you will agree an important one,' he said confidently as he led the way into the heart of the city on foot, having parked the Aston Martin close enough to her Mini to make it look shabbier than ever. Bath looked beautiful in the dark, lights from the shops brightening the cobbled side streets. 'A few changes and it could kick-start your relationship. Ed won't know what's hit him.'

'I've never had any complaints before,' Lucy pointed out. 'In fact, Ed's really good about complimenting me on my appearance. He always notices when I get my hair cut. He likes the way I look.'

Gabriel nodded admiringly. 'He's got his head screwed on, I'll give him that. Always stick to the rule.'

'What rule?'

'You know, if you can't say anything good, then don't say anything. She always looks beautiful, especially in the morning, and if she ever asks you if something makes her look big the answer is always no.'

'Even if it does?'

'Especially if it does.'

Lucy stared at him. 'Is there really this underlying theme of men playing some kind of game with us or are you just messing about?'

She sounded shocked and he slowed his pace to a stroll and looked at her with a grin. 'Maybe I'm overstating it a bit,' he said. Then he raised an eyebrow as he apparently debated the question to himself. 'Though not that much. There *is* something of an unwritten rule for men.'

She looked at him quizzically.

'You learn about it as you go along. It's not worth the grief sometimes to be brutally honest so you tell her what she wants to hear and then enjoy your quiet life. Men don't notice what women wear half as much as other women do.'

'In that case what the hell is the point of us being here?' God, he could be exasperating at times.

'Because we want Ed to sit up and take notice, don't we? Look at you through fresh eyes. And the easiest way to make a man do a double take is with your appearance, right?'

Gabriel dragged her by the arm into the beautiful old building that housed Jolly's department store. Designer and high street in one vast place, with chandeliers and lots of steps up and down to different departments. As they stepped out of the lift and walked into the lusciously carpeted personal shopping suite Lucy was surprised to see him kiss the cheek of the impeccably dressed assistant who greeted them. Surely that was a bit overfamiliar, wasn't it?

'Lucy, this is Amanda,' Gabriel said.

Lucy nodded uncertainly at the perfectly groomed blonde woman in her understated suit and heels.

'Amanda, thanks so much for fitting us in,' he said warmly, and led the way into the suite, walking next to the woman as Lucy lagged a few paces behind them feeling drab in her jeans and sweater. 'Getting married soon, could do with a makeover…' she heard him say and her eyes widened. What a cheek!

Amanda showed them both to a huge squashy leather sofa, and then disappeared through a side door. The moment they were sitting down and she was out of earshot, Lucy elbowed Gabriel hard in the ribs.

'Ow!'

'Serves you right!' she said in an angry stage whisper. 'Could do with a makeover? There's nothing wrong with the way I look!'

'Calm down, Lu.' He held his hands up in

mock surrender. 'I'm just keeping her sweet. Just making sure she realises we're not, you know, *together.* Do you have any idea how booked up this place gets? Told you I'd call in a favour. I knew Amanda would squeeze us in, time being of the essence and everything.' He winked at her.

She rolled her eyes skyward in exasperation. 'You mean I'll be getting dress tips from one of your conquests? You must be joking!'

He made an urgent shushing gesture, which infuriated her all the more. 'Keep your voice down! She's not a conquest, since you ask, but she is a friend of a friend and—'

'Oh, great. She just isn't a conquest *yet,* then. Big difference.'

'Will you just chill out? She's excellent at her job and you want to try on some new stuff. Where's the problem?'

She shook her head impatiently at him and then pasted a polite smile on her face as Amanda reappeared with an armful of clothes and began hanging them on a rail at the side of the room.

She threw a glance Lucy's way and smiled. 'Size eight,' she said. 'Possibly a ten in jeans and definitely petite.' It was a statement, not a question.

Lucy nodded in admiration. 'You're good,' she had to admit.

Amanda came over to the sofa and smiled at them. 'That's what I'm paid for,' she said. 'Follow me, Lucy. I'll pull some things together for you to try and we can get an idea of what suits your body type best and what colours work well for you, that kind of thing.' She shifted her gaze to Gabriel. 'Make yourself comfortable, Gabriel. There'll be some drinks along in a minute.' She flashed him a brilliant smile. Gabriel smiled back at her and stretched out in the corner of the sofa, his arms behind his head.

Lucy followed Amanda into the curtained fitting-room section of the suite. None of the horror of the communal changing room here, thankfully. No desperate shrugging into clothes and deliberately avoiding eye contact with everyone else, all of them doing exactly the same thing. Instead a large, private square room with a clothing rail down one side and a mirror down the other. A much larger bank of mirrors was placed outside, of course, by the sofas, where you could have a three-hundred-sixty-degree view of yourself as you walked around, and where your guest could watch and give you feedback. In her case that meant Gabriel. She felt absurdly shy. It was ridiculous, she told herself. She'd known Gabe all her life practically. And anyway, it shouldn't matter what he thought about how she looked; this was all aimed at Ed, after all. She shrugged out of her plain T-shirt and took the first item off the hanger.

Gabriel surreptitiously got out his smartphone. Not entirely to check his emails, but also to avoid conversing with Amanda, who drifted back to him on a cloud of her own perfume every time she left Lucy to change into some new item. Attractive as she was, he had no time for a fling right now. Another assistant had briefly appeared and deposited a tray of sparkling wine and nibbles to one side of him.

He looked up at the swish of the curtain as Lucy walked self-consciously out into the centre of the mirrors. She was wearing a long black skirt and a flowing blouse over it with a busy floral print. He could tell just by looking at her that she liked it. Of course she did. It could have been from her own wardrobe.

Amanda was shaking her head. 'Pretty, but it totally drowns your figure, there's no definition there.' She deftly grabbed a handful of blouse and held it against the small of Lucy's back. 'See how much better it would look if it was nipped in at the waist? I'd like to see you in something a bit more eye-catching, too.'

'Amanda's totally right,' Gabriel piped up, and the stylist flushed with pleasure. Two birds with one stone, he congratulated himself. Look interested and keep Amanda on side at the same time.

There was a ratcheting sound as Amanda expertly flipped through the clothes on the rail. 'Something a bit more tailored,' she was saying. 'You're so tiny you just look swamped in these floaty designs.'

Lucy disappeared back behind the curtain. Gabriel absently flipped through an email about a case he'd just taken on. It looked as if it might be more complicated than he'd first thought, he'd better request some more information. Then, glancing briefly back up, he froze, the phone held aloft. When had Lucy got legs like that?

Lucy had a fragile silhouette, making a mockery of the fact that her life revolved around the creation of cakes and pastries. But rather than make her look skinny as loose clothes often did, the scarlet shirt she wore now clung in all the right places. The nipped-in cut showed off her tiny waist and with it she was wearing a pair of figure-hugging black cigarette pants. His mouth felt suddenly dry, as if it were full of sawdust, and he automatically took a swig of the very inferior sparkling wine.

'Those trousers aren't really Lucy's style,' he heard himself say. 'Tell her, Lu, you run a bakery. That kind of thing isn't practical.'

Both women totally ignored him. 'Try them with these, Lucy,' Amanda said. 'More definition and height.'

Lucy stepped into the nude platform heels and he inadvertently pressed 'Send' on the email he'd only half written. The extra height from the shoes made her legs go on for ever. She was looking at him for approval and he floundered to get the words out.

'Very nice,' was the best he could manage.

'Perhaps some evening wear next…' Amanda said and held a gold satin dress up against Lucy. Even on its hanger he could see it fell a good three inches above the knee and his heart lurched involuntarily in his chest.

'That'll never work,' he remarked.

Amanda turned to him in exasperation. 'A

bit more positive input wouldn't go amiss, Gabriel. Know a lot about styling someone, do you?'

'It's all because he likes to go out with stereotypes, Amanda,' Lucy said loudly, making sure Gabriel could hear her. '"Arm candy" is the phrase, I think. He likes his women to wear killer heels and fitted tops and skinny jeans, don't you, Gabe?' she teased him. 'I'm the polar opposite of your type, aren't I? How could I ever look good in something your exes would wear?'

She turned to Amanda. 'I'm not really a woman in Gabriel's eyes,' she said. 'More of a female-yet-one-of-the-lads hybrid.'

'A ladette?' Amanda grinned, glancing smugly at her own very satisfactory feminine reflection in the mirror behind Lucy's.

'Yes, a ladette! Exactly!' Lucy laughed at him from across the room. 'You'd no sooner put me in that dress than you would one of your rugby mates, eh, Gabe?'

'Don't be ridiculous. I just meant it's… well…it's different from the kind of thing you usually wear, that's all.' He struggled to justify himself.

'That's the whole point of a styling session—to push boundaries and try new things so you can emphasise your good points,' Amanda pointed out knowledgably. He was beginning to actively dislike the woman. He couldn't remember the last time he'd felt this uncomfortable in female company.

He was glad when the pair of them disappeared behind the curtain. He hadn't counted on this. He'd expected Lucy to have a fun hour or so trying things on while he did a bit of work. He hadn't banked on Amanda pushing clothes on her that his own girlfriends might wear. His Lucy most certainly did not look like girlfriend material in his head and she shouldn't be looking like it in reality.

The curtain swished back again and she sashayed out towards him, her confidence growing before his eyes. The gold dress flowed against her skin and clung to her every contour. The mirrors made it worse—he could see her from every angle. He tugged at his collar, which suddenly felt unbearably tight, and beads of sweat broke out on his brow. Lucy had curves. She had a tiny waist and long, long legs, and skin that was the colour of double cream. She smiled at him, waiting for an opinion, and all he could feel was shock that she could look so grown-up, so…sexy. He felt a sudden rush of longing deep inside and his face must have given it away because a puzzled expression crossed her face.

'What's wrong? Don't you like it?'

He looked at her face, her eyes wide. His mind whirled. He recognised this feeling of course; he had it all the time. Pretty much whenever an attractive woman came into his field of vision. He just wasn't used to having it about Lucy. In his mind he had her very comfortably pigeonholed as Best Friend, and he'd known her for so long he realised he never even usually noticed how she looked. It seemed the wake-up call planned for Ed was working on him, too.

You're jealous! The thought came from nowhere with the force of a sledgehammer, making him feel dizzy. This was just about Lucy getting married ruining their friendship, wasn't it? *Was it really?* He mentally shook himself, noticing her crestfallen expression, and forced himself to speak.

'You look beautiful, Lu. I love it.'

'You had a weird look on your face.'

'I guess I'm more used to seeing you in T-shirts and jeans.'

'I think it would benefit from some good lingerie,' Amanda interjected, holding up a beautiful black bra and knickers set, adorned with delicate silk and lace. 'What size are you, Lucy?'

Gabriel almost choked on the foul sparkling wine. He had to get out of here. Now.

'I have to, er, make a move,' he blurted out suddenly, holding up his phone like an idiot. 'Urgent. Work thing. Can't be helped. Sorry.' Aware he was now gabbling, he snatched up his jacket to create a diversion.

Lucy looked momentarily surprised, but, delighted as she was with her transformation, her attention was quickly diverted by the clothes Amanda was holding. She walked briefly over to him, the heels emphasising her legs even more. He fought to keep his eyes off them. 'No problem, Gabe, I'll call you later,' she said. She flashed him an excited smile. 'Thanks for organising this—you're such a good mate!' She looked up into his face for a moment and her smile faltered. 'You know, you work too hard. You have dark shadows under your eyes.' She ran a fingertip across his left cheekbone and he felt his skin prickle deliciously as if it might burst into flames at her touch. Her scent, something light and floral, enveloped him. He felt as if his senses were sharpened to a needle point, as if every nerve in his body were standing on end.

Amanda saw him to the lift, leaning in close enough to whisper in his ear. 'Call me,' she said, giving him an inviting smile. He was glad when the metal doors slid shut between them.

He left the store as fast as he could, relishing the fresh air on his burning face as he walked to the car. As he drove home he barely saw the road, barely noticed the other cars or people. One person filled his head. This was a whole different ball game. And he had no idea how he was supposed to play it.

CHAPTER FOUR

'SO YOU went clothes shopping with a woman, what, have you lost your mind?'

Gabriel slung a towel round his neck and took a swig from his water bottle. Playing a couple of games of squash with Joe, a work colleague, he intended to beat the tension out of himself with physical exertion. So far it wasn't working.

He hadn't been able to focus now for two days. Whenever he tried, his mind was invaded by Lucy: how she'd looked, how she smelled, how her skin felt when she held his arm. He couldn't remember a woman making him feel like this since Alison, and even she was now beginning to become a blur. To his dismay it was beginning to dawn on him that the reason he didn't want Lucy to get married had less to do with the impact on their friendship and more to do with the fact she was marrying someone else.

You want her for yourself, his mind whispered, and it seemed he was powerless to crush that thought. When he remembered Alison now his mind seemed to have sideslipped into comparison mode, where her smile was lovely but Lucy's smile made every cell in his body tingle. Alison's blonde hair had been silky and pretty but Lucy's insane curls made him want to tangle his hands in them and never let go.

'Not in the sense you think,' he panted in reply. He leaned against the wall and towelled the sweat from his face. 'She's going to propose to her boyfriend. There's some kind of leap year thing where women are supposed to be allowed to propose marriage instead of men. I was helping her pick some clothes out.'

To his surprise, Joe nodded. 'My sister did it. She asked her husband to marry her eight years ago on February twenty-ninth. Poor guy didn't stand a chance.'

Gabriel ran his hands distractedly through his hair. 'Thing is, Lucy's a friend. More of a sister really—we grew up together. But watching her showing off in these clothes… I never really noticed before just how stunning she is.

Now I can't stop thinking about her. And I'm meant to be helping her plan this proposal to the guy in less than two weeks' time. Right now I feel like I want to knock his head off if he goes anywhere near her.'

Joe stared at him as if he were mad. 'You are kidding me, right? You need to see the new girl in the office. That'll soon get your mind back on track.'

Gabriel buried his face for a moment in the towel. He felt no spark of interest whatsoever in the new girl in the typing pool. But two weeks ago he would have already been dating her. He felt as if his life had been turned upside down.

'Maybe you're right,' he said, more to placate Joe than anything. 'I haven't dated for a few weeks. Every waking moment's been taken up with the Pryor case and this thing with Lucy.'

'Course I am.' Joe clapped him encouragingly on the shoulder as they walked back onto the court. 'Get the proposal out of the way and things will get back to normal. She'll have a wedding to plan and, trust me, you don't want to get within a hundred miles of a woman doing that.'

Gabriel picked up his racket and smacked the squash ball with every ounce of strength he had. The thought of Lucy marrying Ed was beginning to make him feel ill.

'Lucy, darling, you look as beautiful as ever. It's so good to see you.' Gabriel's mother Elizabeth swept Lucy into a tight warm hug, and Lucy momentarily closed her eyes so as to soak up every drop of love in it. She thought for the hundredth time what a lovely person Elizabeth was and felt that age-old pang of childhood jealousy against Gabriel for having such a supportive close family when her own home life had been such a shambles.

'These are for you.' Lucy handed over the white cardboard box she had brought with her. Elizabeth lifted the lid and exclaimed delightedly at the sight of the cake selection inside. Billowing swirls of jewel-coloured meringue nestled alongside delicately decorated cupcakes.

'Lucy, they're marvellous. Although just one of them is more pudding than I normally eat in a week! You are kind. Gabriel's told me all about how well you are doing. We love hearing about the shop—I'm so pleased it's such a success.'

Lucy followed her as she led the way through the cool hallway to the large kitchen at the back of the manor. She met Gabriel's eyes behind his mother's back. He shrugged apologetically but she shook her head at him and smiled. She adored Elizabeth, and thought it was wonderful to have a mother to whom you could entrust all the tiny details of your life. Her own mother had been totally preoccupied by her own life and problems and Lucy had never been able to confide in her. The kitchen was warm from the Aga with a huge scrubbed wooden table and a kind-faced woman of about fifty preparing the lunch.

'This is Angela,' Elizabeth said. The woman turned from peeling vegetables at the sink and smiled at them. 'Angela's an absolute treasure,' she confided to Lucy as they returned to the sitting room, having deposited the cakes in the kitchen. 'Keeps the house perfect and cooks for us when we need her to. Like today. I'm more than capable of rustling up scrambled eggs for Gordon and myself, but it's such a joy to have someone else cook the more demanding meals now.'

The lunch proved to be delicious, the multi-tasking Angela serving them all as effortlessly as she had apparently cooked the meal. Lucy realised she was having a wonderful time; she really did feel as if she'd come home. She supposed Gabe must feel like this every time he came—how lucky he was.

'How are your parents, Lucy dear? Do you see much of them?' Lucy felt a stab of embarrassment that Elizabeth knew what a nightmare her mother and father were.

'Not really. Christmas and birthday cards, you know. The occasional phone call.' Exactly the way she wanted it. She had total control now over her own life, the polar opposite to her awful childhood years. 'My mother's in Las Vegas now with her latest husband. Number three. And my father's up in Birmingham. A friend of his offered him a job. Nothing like the work he did for you, of course.'

Elizabeth nodded politely.

'Hospital porter, I think he is now,' Lucy added vaguely. 'It suits me, to be honest, that they've both moved away. I have my own life now and that's the way I want it.' She smiled at Elizabeth. 'It's lovely coming here, though. Reminds me of the fun Gabriel and I had as kids.' She'd changed the subject swiftly and effortlessly. God knew she'd had enough practice at avoiding discussing her parents.

After lunch, Gabriel and his father had coffee in the drawing room, and Elizabeth asked Lucy to accompany her on a walk in the gardens. They strolled arm in arm.

'It's looking lovely.' Lucy admired the beds and the well-kept lawn. She could almost see herself and Gabriel kicking the old football around here when they were little. There were some fantastic trees to climb on the estate too. She smiled to herself. She'd been such a tomboy.

'How kind of you to say so, dear. I don't do so much of it myself these days, of course. Gordon has a man come in a few times a week in the spring and summer. Keeps it up together. Less to do in the winter of course.'

They walked on in silence for a moment. Elizabeth seemed faintly tense and Lucy couldn't help thinking she'd asked her to come for a walk deliberately so that they could talk privately. She had no idea why that might be.

'Is something wrong?' she asked curiously.

Elizabeth smiled at her. 'Not especially, dear. I just wondered how Gabriel is. I know he tells us he's fine but I can never really get any information out of him. I was hoping you could give me some insight. Do you think he's happy?' She sighed. 'We don't see as much of him as we'd like these days.'

Lucy looked at her in surprise. She'd always thought of Gabriel as very close to his parents.

'Yes, of course he is. He's done so brilliantly at work, you know. He's ahead of his time. He's quite well known in legal circles, I think. And he has an incredibly busy social life.'

Elizabeth didn't miss the implication. 'Still no one special, then.' She sighed again. 'I do worry about him so. When he lost Alison he was still very young. Young enough to start again. She was such a lovely girl, I knew it would take him some time to get over it. But he's never even once brought a girlfriend to meet us since.'

Lucy patted her hand reassuringly, thinking that the word 'lost' just didn't really cover it. It was Elizabeth's shorthand for the fact that Gabriel's first love, his college sweetheart, had died in a car accident the year after they left university. She knew he'd been devastated at the time. But as the years had passed he had never opened up about it beyond the bare facts, not even to her. Eventually he had stopped talking about it altogether and Lucy had taken her cue from him and avoided the subject like the plague for fear of upsetting him. Gabriel behaved as though Alison had never existed at all. Until you took a closer look and realised that he'd simply spent every relationship since making sure nothing like it could ever happen to him again. None of his girlfriends were ever allowed to get close enough for them to mean anything to him. Elizabeth was right: after ten years he really hadn't moved on.

She did her best to be reassuring. 'He'll settle down one day, Elizabeth. I'm sure of it. He just seems…I don't know…happy with the way things are at the moment.'

'You know, Gordon and I always hoped you and he might end up…' Elizabeth spoke wistfully, then quickly pulled herself up short.

Lucy jumped a little, as if she'd taken a whiff of smelling salts. She felt the heat of an unexpected blush creep slowly upwards from her collar and was momentarily flustered. A long-buried memory surfaced and she tried her best to push it back to the depths of her mind from where it had come. The very idea of her having a relationship with Gabriel should be laughable. She was sure Gabe would laugh out loud at the suggestion. She certainly shouldn't be having this reaction. Heart rate increasing, temperature rising. She felt embarrassed and hoped fervently that Elizabeth wouldn't pick up on how agitated she was.

The truth was there had been a time, long ago, when her feelings of friendship for Gabriel had become something more. Only in her mind, of course, never his. She pondered for a moment that you never realised the true value of something until it had gone. She had learned that when Gabriel left for university all those years ago. Up until then he'd been hers. Two years older. Protector. Brother. His mother had a dislike of boarding school, instead sending Gabe to a nearby prep school. Lucy, of course, had gone to the local primary school. Their education was a world apart, just like their houses, their parents, their backgrounds, but none of it had mattered to them. They had remained close despite and, she thought now, perhaps because of their differences. Each was everything the other needed. She had been an antidote to his stuffy school atmosphere and her sense of fun had brought him respite from the intense studying it had demanded.

He had been her port in a storm. The rows and upheaval at home had gradually worsened through her teens and she'd found herself relying on him more and more. His reasoned thinking had encouraged her to consider the long term, to believe that it wouldn't be like this for ever, stuck in a village in the middle of nowhere with her warring parents and no means of escape. One day she would have her own life and she would be free.

Gabriel had never been taken away from her until he'd accepted a place to study law at Oxford. Her initial delight for him had given way to a growing, gnawing dread as the day had approached when he would start his first term. She hadn't realised how heavily she'd come to depend on him. She was used to barely a day going by without speaking to him.

She'd missed him painfully, dreadfully, and she'd imagined he must be feeling the same way. Her sense of embarrassment now was rooted in the memory of how in his absence he'd begun to take on more than just the role of friend in her mind. She'd begun to fantasise about them being together as a couple, falling in love, having a future together. On his brief weekend visits home his touch had begun to make her skin tingle and her heart had begun to race when he entered a room. Greedy for his time and attention, she'd hung on his every word.

'I'm sorry, dear.' Elizabeth spoke apologetically, bringing Lucy sharply back to the present. 'It's nothing to do with us, of course. It's simply that, well, I remember the first time he met you, knocking on the front door, only about six you were, looking for your lost kitten. Gabriel must have been about nine. It was that really hot summer.'

She was relieved at the change of subject. This part of memory lane she could cope with. 'Sooty,' she remembered. 'I was beside myself. We'd only just moved in and my mother had let him out before he'd had a chance to get used to the house.'

'Gabriel spent the entire afternoon searching with you, until you found him, remember?'

'He'd just got shut inside one of the outbuildings.' She smiled at the memory. 'I was frantic.'

'All Gabriel wanted to do from that moment on was look after you and make you happy. I've watched him over the years and he's never changed. You've always been so close, I suppose I hoped it might one day become more than just a friendship.'

'We're more like brother and sister really,' Lucy said, firmly, for her own benefit as much as Elizabeth's. She cuddled closer to the old lady. 'I was always so jealous of him when I was little. I wanted to be part of your family, too. I was so happy up here at the big house. And he's always been there for me. He's never once let me down.'

Elizabeth smiled at her. 'How is your young man, dear?' she asked politely. Lucy felt a rush of sudden guilt. Her mind had been full of Gabriel and talking about their shared past had made her feel happy and nostalgic, but also unsettled. She could kick herself for feeling so girly and flustered at the suggestion of them ever being a couple. She hadn't spared a thought for Ed all day. But that didn't necessarily mean she was betraying him, did it? It was just this place, nothing more. Being here was bound to stir up her feelings. Her past here had been so turbulent, it would surely be strange if it didn't evoke strong emotions.

'Ed? He's well, thank you.' She felt a sudden desire to confide in Elizabeth, to affirm to her, and perhaps also to herself, that romantic thoughts in her head were linked only to him and not for a second to Gabriel. 'Between you and me I was hoping we might settle down and get married, but he doesn't seem to take the hint. Gabriel thinks he's lazy and doesn't do enough to look after me, but you know how overprotective he can be.'

Elizabeth sighed. She was quiet for a moment before saying, 'Relationships, Lucy, *good* relationships, don't come along by accident in my experience. You have to work at them. Both of you. One of you doing everything just isn't enough—it has to be a partnership. Gordon and I have had our ups and downs—goodness, we've been married a long time now. But we've always pulled together. He's a pain sometimes but I wouldn't be without him, not for anything.'

Lucy grinned.

'Only you can say if this Ed puts enough effort in. You make sure he's the right one for you. You deserve nothing less.'

Shortly afterwards they returned to the house and Lucy was glad when she and Gabriel left for Bath. Talking to Elizabeth had stirred her mind up far too much for her to relax on the journey home. She sat in silence in the car next to Gabriel, the memory coming unbidden to her in all its clarity of the first time she'd met Alison, and her face flushed with mortification as she remembered the circumstances of that meeting.

If Gabriel had guessed how she was feeling after he left for uni, he never let on, just behaving the way he always did, full of news about his course, his new life and his new friends. Yet her delusions had grown until she'd believed herself to be in love with him. The brotherly hugs he gave her and the occasional holding of her hand she'd begun to construe as reciprocation of her fledgling feelings, and she would lay awake at night thinking about him.

She blushed as she remembered her behaviour. A typical stupid teenage crush, that was what it had been. And she'd come so close to Gabe finding out about it that the memory alone still made her heart hammer and her cheeks burn.

Shortly into Gabriel's second term, his visits home began to dwindle and he was useless at keeping in touch. Lucy phoned him so often that she later realised she must have been becoming a pest. She recalled now that there were many occasions when his housemates had told her he was out. With the benefit of age and maturity she now saw that he was probably fed up with her constant contact and was trying, albeit gently, to avoid her.

Convinced Gabriel would feel the same about her if she could just see him and declare her feelings, she'd decided on impulse to visit him one day, when missing him had all become too much. She remembered gazing out of the window of the bus from the train station and thinking to herself how busy and vibrant Oxford seemed compared to the Cotswold villages she was used to. She remembered the butterflies in her stomach on the bus to his digs as the miles between them fell away…

She grinned as she climbed the steps to his front door, thinking how pleased he would be to see her. She was wearing a new sea-green top, which she knew brought out the colour of her eyes, and she'd spent ages trying to get her hair to behave itself. But the broad smile she'd been unable to keep off her face dwindled as the door opened. Not Gabriel but a slender and impossibly pretty blonde girl.

The girl smiled kindly at Lucy. 'Can I help you?'

Lucy craned to see behind her into the hall-

way. Maybe she'd got the wrong house. But before she had time to say anything Gabriel himself appeared. He came to the door and suddenly she felt light-headed. She didn't look up into the gorgeous slate-grey eyes and walk into his embrace, the way she'd planned to all the way here. She couldn't tear her eyes away from his arm, which slid easily around the blonde girl's waist as he nestled close enough to her to enable him to see around the door.

'Lucy!' he exclaimed, in obvious surprise. She noticed he didn't let go of the girl as he opened the door wider. Instead he slipped his hand into hers and they surveyed her together. Lucy felt her heart twist in her chest and she swallowed hard to stop the burning sensation that began at the back of her throat. She had to find a way out of this.

'Surprise!' she said on impulse, weakly shrugging her shoulders. She was agonisingly aware suddenly of how idiotic she must seem to Gabriel just turning up like this unannounced, like some runaway.

'Lucy, this is a lovely surprise, but does your dad know you're here?' His unintended patronising concern made her face flame with humiliation. She was sixteen after all, not a child.

Before she could speak, he addressed the blonde girl. 'Ali, this is Lucy.' Lucy couldn't seem to look away from the entwined hands. 'I told you about her. Kind of like my baby sister from back home.'

Alison smiled at her. 'Hi, Lucy,' she said warmly. 'It's good to meet you. Gabriel's mentioned you a few times. It's nice to put a face to a name.'

A few times. *Gabriel hadn't been out of her thoughts for longer than a few minutes these past weeks, but he clearly hadn't been dwelling on her in the same way.*

She was snatched back from her thoughts of the past when Gabriel touched her hand briefly before replacing his on the steering wheel. 'You're quiet, Lu. Everything all right?'

'Fine. I'm just tired.' Her hand tingled at his touch and she stared down at it. *Oh, what is happening here?* She felt the blush creep up her face, as if Oxford had happened yesterday, and she was grateful that his attention was focused on the road so he wouldn't notice. She remembered that she only managed to stomach an hour or so of seeing the two of them together. Alison was studying medicine and they both had rooms in the shared house. She could see they were besotted with each other. Lucy had been so full of excitement at seeing him, believing him to be unknowingly in love with her, expecting to fall into his arms as it all became clear to him. Well, she'd certainly found him in love, just not with her.

She'd managed to hold it together at the house but she'd sobbed her heart out all the way back to Gloucestershire on the bus and then the train. The only comfort she'd had was that she'd stopped short of making a fool of herself by exposing her feelings to him. *His baby sister.* It stung. She was so hurt and humiliated that her first instinct had been to avoid him completely. She stopped calling him after that. But she quickly realised how stupid she was to think she could cut him from her life. She needed him far too much for that.

So when he'd brought Alison back to the manor she hadn't stayed away. It had crushed her to see how happy he was. It became clear that their relationship was not going to be over quickly. That it was a proper, adult relationship. Alison completed him in a way Lucy never had. They'd been all things to each other for so long and now she wasn't enough for him any more. And she began to see with growing, frightening clarity that there could very easily be no place for her at all in all this. She was totally dispensable in the face of his perfect future with Alison. And under threat of losing him altogether, she'd made a decision. Better to keep him as a friend than to lose him completely from her life because of her own stupid pride.

And so it was that she had played the part of childhood best friend until it became no longer an act and was second nature to her. In the years since she had managed to convince herself that her behaviour had been nothing more than a ridiculous teenage crush, brought on by the sudden gap he had left in her life when he went to university, combined with the worsening hell that was her inescapable home life.

Since that awful moment at sixteen she'd never again allowed herself to consider Gabriel as more than a friend, a brother, but that apparently hadn't stopped his parents doing just that. Thinking about it now made her feel suddenly hot, as if she'd walked into a sauna. Before she could stop herself she was trying the idea for size in her head. Her stomach fluttered and she covered it angrily with her hands. It had been a *crush.* Nothing more.

Then why did you blush when his mother mentioned it? She fought that thought with all her might. She couldn't imagine a circumstance in which she would lay their friendship on the line. Gabriel was useless at relationships; they rarely lasted longer than a month. He just didn't seem to have it in him since Alison died. Lucy's talk today with his mother had highlighted that more strongly than ever. What if they got together and it didn't work out? For the first time since she was sixteen she considered what it would be like to have a life without Gabe in it, and it shocked her to the core now as it had then. She would never allow that to happen.

'Come on up.'

The moment the buzzer sounded as Lucy unlocked the outer door of her building, Gabriel shoved the door open and leapt up the stairs two at a time. The door of her flat was shut, which struck him as a little unusual because she usually left it ajar for him when she buzzed him up. The reason became clear when he gave it a brief double tap.

'You can't come in!' a determined but high voice called out. It was followed by fumbling sounds as the door was opened and Lucy appeared in the gap with an apologetic expression.

'Sorry, Gabe. This one thinks he's Spiderman. I had to keep the door shut in case he wandered out looking for Dr Octopus.'

Opening the door wider, Gabriel saw a small figure dressed in a Spiderman costume standing behind Lucy, who was looking red and flustered. Her unruly hair was even more uncontrollably curly than ever. Unable to stop himself grinning, Gabriel knelt down to one knee so his eyes were level with the mask on the child's face. A pair of alert brown eyes blinked at him through the eyeholes.

'Hello, Spiderman,' he said. 'I'm Lucy's friend, Gabriel.' He held out his hand and the child shook it solemnly.

'Shall we go into the living room?' Lucy said impatiently from above them, and led the way without waiting for a response. 'Steven, I'll put your Fireman Sam DVD on.' As Gabriel caught up with her she added over her shoulder, 'Thank goodness you've arrived. Back-up at last!'

It was Monday night. The day after their lunch in Gloucestershire. Gabriel had taken advantage of the car journey home to organise yet another opportunity to spend time with Lucy. At this rate she and Ed would grow apart through lack of contact without his having to do or say anything at all. When Steven was settled in front of the television with a cup of milk, Gabriel joined Lucy in the kitchen. She made them each a mug of coffee and they watched Steven through the open door as he sat perfectly still, his attention focused on the TV screen.

'He's Sophie's boy,' Lucy said. 'You know, she works part-time in the shop?'

Gabriel nodded, continuing to watch the child. 'What's he doing here?'

'Sophie's mum was rushed to hospital this afternoon with chest pains. I think there's some kind of history of heart problems. Sophie is her only family, so I said I'd have Steven overnight while she's at the hospital. He's been here since six.'

'Where's Ed?'

She made an impatient noise and Gabriel glanced at her in surprise. 'He made an early exit to go for extra football training. To be honest he looked pleased to be going. I don't think the prospect of entertaining Steven was his idea of a good time.' She ran a flustered hand through her hair. 'It doesn't matter what I say, he refuses to take the Spiderman suit off. He's going to have to sleep in it at this rate.'

As they watched Steven lifted the mask off his face just enough to fit the rim of his cup of milk underneath it.

'I mean, he's only four,' Lucy said, almost to herself. 'How hard can it be?'

Gabriel burst out laughing. 'For goodness' sake, Lu, lighten up. Remember when we were kids and you practically lived in that tutu one summer? All kids like dressing up. Just let him get on with it.'

She looked at him crossly. 'I don't mean that, you idiot. I admit it's a bit weird not seeing his face but I actually think the superhero outfit is quite cute. I mean he keeps asking me about his gran and I don't know what to tell him.' She lowered her voice. 'I got the impression it was touch and go and I don't want to give Steven false hope.'

She looked up at him worriedly and he put an arm around her and gave her a reassuring squeeze.

'Don't worry. It'll be OK. We can sit with him together and I'll distract him until bedtime. Then tomorrow Sophie can take over and talk to him.'

She smiled up at him, relieved, and he realised how happy it made him just to help her out with the slightest thing. It always had done, no matter how old they were. He felt protective of her in a way he never had about anyone else.

An hour later Lucy watched from the doorway, her empty coffee mug held against her chest unnoticed. She was totally absorbed by the sight of Gabriel playing with Steven and she couldn't stop herself comparing it with Ed's sharp disappearance when she'd told him Steven would be staying. It hadn't occurred to him that she might need a hand, had it? But Gabriel hadn't batted an eyelid. She realised, in all the years she'd known Gabe, she'd never watched him interact with children before. Not so surprising, she supposed. He was an only child like her, so there were no nieces or nephews to get involved with, and his friends were very much like him. Generally they were single sports-obsessed professionals with no fixed girlfriend. Yet to see him now you'd think Gabriel came into contact with four-year-olds every day of the week. She felt a tug at her heart and shook herself. She had deliberately banished those ridiculous feelings from yesterday's lunch. It was just cold feet about making things permanent with Ed, that was all.

'I'm not really just Lucy's friend, Gabriel, you know,' she heard him telling the child. 'I just let Lucy think that—it's part of my cover. I'm really Sonic Man. I can hear things that happen miles and miles away. That's my super power, just like you can climb walls and spin webs.'

Lucy watched the small dark head looking up at Gabriel. 'My nana's in the hospital,' she heard Steven say in a small voice. 'She got taken away in an ambulance.'

'I know she did,' Gabriel said. 'Lucy told me. Your nana's very ill, Steven, but they're going to do the best they can to make her better. And she's in the best place she possibly could be. There are lots of brilliant doctors there. I'm sure your mum will call soon, so try not to worry, OK?' He smiled at Steven. 'Shall we ask Lucy for a biscuit before you go up to bed?'

Lucy stepped back from the door in the nick

of time as Steven pelted through to the kitchen looking less agitated than he had done since he'd arrived. Gabriel followed him and she shot him a grateful smile over Steven's head. He'd made more progress with the child in ten minutes than she'd made in three hours. Steven had refused to say anything to her about his grandmother, however hard she'd tried. She itched to talk to Gabriel about it but made herself wait until Steven was settled in bed. Steven insisted on Gabriel tucking him in, and she made more coffee while she waited for him.

She held one of the mugs out as Gabriel re-entered the room. 'Here you go, Sonic Man. I think you've earned it.'

Gabriel looked mildly embarrassed. He took the mug from her and sat down on the sofa. 'You were listening,' he said.

'It was sweet,' she insisted, smiling at him. 'He's a million times happier now. I know it might be bad news tomorrow but at least he'll get a good night's sleep.' She took a sip of her drink, watching him over the rim of the mug. 'I had no idea you were such a natural with kids.'

A pause. 'Am I?' he said lightly. 'I really hadn't given it a thought.' He seemed to be avoiding meeting her eyes but she wasn't going to be put off that easily. Their recent discussions about her own relationship had made her realise that they never discussed his. Well, she corrected herself, only in terms of her ribbing him about being a playboy and teasing him that he couldn't remember the name of his latest conquest. He never ever talked about how he felt in relation to any of them. She couldn't believe she'd been wondering whether she and Gabe could ever be a couple. Especially when she already had her relationship for life all worked out. Perhaps she should try and encourage him to find someone more permanent, too. As she was his best friend that should be her role, not this mad daydreaming about something that could never and should never happen.

'Yes,' she said pointedly. 'You are. You'd make a great dad. Don't you ever think about that? About settling down and having a family?' She watched him closely for his reaction.

He stood up and made a move towards the kitchen. 'Got any biscuits or cakes, Lu? I'm starving.'

'In the cupboard behind the door,' she called after him, and waited determinedly until he returned with a handful of biscuits.

He sat down again and ran a hand distractedly through his thick dark hair. ‘So, have you given any more thought to how you’re going to propose to Ed?’ He offered her one of his biscuits with a smile.

She flapped a dismissive hand at him. ‘Don’t change the subject,’ she said purposefully.

‘I’m not!’ he protested. ‘Wasn’t your proposal the whole reason for me coming over?’

‘Technically, yes, but since you’ve been relishing pulling my lovelife apart and sticking it under a microscope, I think I deserve to be allowed to question you for a change.’ She ignored his frown and carried on. ‘I want an answer. Where do you see your future? Do you want a family one day, or do you plan to just cruise on through life rudderless?’

Gabriel gave a cold little laugh. ‘I don’t want to talk about it, Lucy, so let’s just get back on task, shall we?’ His grey eyes, normally full of warmth for her, flashed dark and dangerous.

Lucy pretended not to notice how agitated he was becoming. His reluctance to talk only spurred her on. She knew, of course, why he was so on edge. She was skirting around the issue of Alison. But after talking to his mother she couldn’t help thinking it would be for his own good if Gabriel did open up about Alison and how he felt. After the embarrassment of that day in Oxford, she hadn't permitted herself the easy luxury of disliking Alison. She couldn't let herself feel jealous because that would be to admit that she cared. Alison had been a sweet and kind person and Lucy had genuinely liked her.

'Don't brush me off like that, Gabe.' She leaned forward in her chair and grabbed his hand impulsively. He looked down at it, concealing his face from her so she couldn't read any emotion. 'Don't you think it's time you let go?' she said gently.

He didn't look up and his voice was mechanically neutral. 'I don't know what you're talking about.' He pulled his hand away from hers and she was suddenly left clutching fresh air. She looked down at her empty fingers and shook her head. No way was she letting this slide now.

'Yes, you do,' she said, firmly and deliberately.

He still didn't look up.

'You forget, Gabriel, that I knew Alison, too,' she said softly, as much to herself as to him. 'She was lovely, Gabe. Women can be really gossipy, you know, really catty sometimes. But not her. And she was never once bothered by me—do you remember that? All your new conquests can't stand you having a female best mate, but Alison just saw me as someone to go shopping with, who she could moan to about your rugby obsession. I can understand why you were so devastated when she died, but do you really think she'd want this? You, the eternal bachelor, never moving on? The Alison I knew would have wanted more for you.'

She paused, wondering if she'd gone too far. *God, Lucy, you never ask him about the girl for nigh on ten years and then put him on the spot. You'll be lucky if he ever speaks to you again. Is that really what you wanted?* For a moment there was silence in the room, and still Gabriel didn't look up at her. He simply stared down at his glass of wine. But then, just as she was wondering if she really should let the subject drop after all, he spoke.

'We talked sometimes about having kids,' he said quietly, almost to himself. She had to strain to pick up on what he was saying because she couldn't see his lips move. 'She always used to say she wanted six. A tribe, she called it.' He uttered a strangled laugh. 'It sounded a good plan to me. I'd always wanted a big family.'

'I never knew that,' Lucy said gently, marvelling that she'd known him most of her life and yet he'd never mentioned it. And worse, she'd never thought to ask him. How shameful that was. 'You never told me.'

'Yeah, well, I didn't want to do any of it without her so there wasn't much point telling you, was there?' he said quietly and glanced up at her for the first time since he'd started talking. His eyes were dry and his voice showed no sign of emotion. Lucy tried to put a finger on how he sounded. *Empty.* He sounded empty.

There was a long pause. Lucy forced herself not to speak, hoping that he would continue. He was looking down at his hands.

'I didn't want to do any of it without Alison,' he said eventually. 'Without her I'd rather not do it at all. I didn't even want to think of having a family, being a husband or a dad, because she was always meant to be part of the deal.'

'And do you still feel like that?' Lucy asked him, biting her lip. For some reason the question seemed incredibly important to her. Out of concern for him, of course, she told herself. Certainly not for her own information. It had no real impact on *her,* after all. She was Gabe's friend, nothing more.

'I don't let myself think about it, so I really wouldn't know.' He glanced up at her for the briefest moment and his expression was one of such suppressed sorrow that she felt her heart constrict inside her chest. Poor Gabriel. So strong and full of life but never really addressing the feelings at the centre of his soul. He'd put his grief in a box ten years ago and thrown away the key. What an absolute tragedy that after all this time he was no closer to moving on and putting what happened to Alison behind him than he had been at the time.

Lucy couldn't bring herself to press him any harder. She decided to ease up, change the subject. *But this is a breakthrough,* she told herself. *Just getting him to discuss it.* She resolved to find a way to help him get over the past and be the complete person she knew he should be. That was what she should be doing, as his friend. That was where her role was in his life. She stood up.

'Tell you what, I'll put some more coffee on.' She smiled at him supportively. 'And then I'll tell you the latest news from Planet Ed. Did I tell you he's bought me Elvis Presley's film collection? As if bombarding me with his music isn't enough, he's decided we can watch them back to back!' She felt the tension in the room lift as Gabriel laughed. She could see he was relieved at the shift in subject. That was enough soul-searching for one night. *But I'm going to bring it up again soon,* she thought. This burial of emotion just wasn't what she wanted for him.

Gabriel let himself into his house on autopilot three hours later. His mind swam. It was the first time he'd discussed Alison with anyone in at least eight years. During that time he'd built a new normality, he'd become so used to sidestepping conversations about her, to avoiding even *thinking* about her, that it had become second nature.

This evening all that had changed. He felt… he struggled to find the correct word…*exposed* was the closest he could get to it. Laid bare. And the person who'd enabled that to happen was the person he was already confused about beyond all reason.

Turning on the lights, he walked purposefully through his sitting room, straight to the desk in the far corner. Opening one of the deep drawers, he rummaged inside it until he found what he was after. He drew out a small book, its slightly rough burgundy cover interrupted by a single word embossed in cream. 'Photos.'

Not allowing himself to pause, he sat down on the nearest chair and rested his fingertips against the cover for a few moments, steeling himself. It had to be six years at least since he'd opened this book. He knew so well what was inside it but he'd deliberately cut those images from his mind. That was why he'd hidden the book away. He didn't want or need tangible reminders of the past; he had enough of a battle keeping the memories inside his head at bay. He gripped the book tighter for a moment, forcing himself to recognise that hiding these reminders from himself was not a healthy way to live.

With a small intake of breath he opened the book and stared down at the first picture before him. A smile touched his lips. Alison with her pale blonde hair smiled back. No tears came to his eyes, no lump constricted his throat. He'd shed all his tears the first year or two after she'd gone. Night after night when sleep refused to give him respite and he was totally immersed in his grief. Now, looking down at the picture, he realised that he *had* moved on in a sense. *Not that Lucy would agree,* he thought wryly. She seemed to believe that serial dating was symptomatic of long-term grief, but she was wrong. He wasn't stuck grieving; he knew that. He'd chosen not to get involved with anyone since because he didn't want to go back to that period of dreadful loss. Not ever again. But the touch of Lucy's hand tonight, the rush of excitement he'd felt when she'd curled her arms around him and kissed him goodbye on the cheek, made him consider for the first time that maybe in denying that closeness with someone he was only living half a life.

For the last ten years his main thought when he met an attractive woman was how many dates it would take to get her into bed. Now perhaps he could begin to contemplate that there could be more to it than that. The only problem was that his inclination to get any closer than that seemed to be conditional on the particular woman he was thinking of. And ever since he'd taken Lucy shopping there had been no one else for him.

He closed the photo album. Was it possible that he'd had feelings for Lucy even before her recent talk of marriage plans? Perhaps. He just hadn't had any reason to give them any credence before. Why should he, when he already had her friendship without having to take the scary step forward to make it into anything more? Why try to fix something that wasn't broken? But now… Now he wasn't sure if her friendship was enough. And that one thing, he supposed, was the strongest indication that he was ready to move on and put the past behind him. Properly behind him, this time. As a gesture to himself, he deliberately didn't rebury the book in the drawer he never looked inside. Instead he left it on top of the desk, where he could see it any time. Where he would see it, often.

He lay awake into the night knowing that Lucy belonged to someone else. All those things she'd said to him, about moving on, finding someone new and having the family he'd chosen to forget he wanted. She meant finding some other girl. Not her. She already had her happy ever after sorted. And after all this time, was he capable of sustaining a proper long-term relationship? Was it a skill that you had to relearn or did it just come back to you, like swimming or driving? His mind swam with confused feelings. He wasn't about to chance his friendship with Lucy by telling her how he felt. Not when he wasn't even sure himself. And definitely not when their friendship might be the biggest casualty if it all went wrong. Turning over in bed, he resolved to keep his feelings well and truly to himself. Maybe if he did that and kept Lucy at arm's length, these new feelings for her would pass. If he could keep some distance between them until her betrothal to Ed was a done deal, he knew he would never compromise her future and maybe then he could finally move forward properly.

CHAPTER FIVE

GABRIEL did a very efficient job of avoiding Lucy for the next couple of days. This was no mean feat based on the fact that Ed seemed to be paying her more attention. Determined to bury her growing feelings for Gabriel and spurred on by the fact that their plan seemed to be working, she was eager to talk to him about the proposal night and in her usual impatient way bombarded him with phone calls trying to arrange just that.

Eventually, with every moment he spent away from her making him more determined to keep out of her way, he'd even begun to convince himself that his new attraction to her was no more than the result of an off-day. It was the shopping trip, he told himself. He'd just been wrong-footed by being forced to focus on her appearance when he'd never had reason to do that before. Hell, as a kid he'd seen her eating mud, hair all over the place, and as an adult staying with him he'd seen her at her worst. That time she'd drunk too much red wine and had spent the night on the bathroom floor throwing up. She'd looked like death the next morning. No, he told himself, he could brush any mad feelings aside. She was still the same old Lucy, no regard for what time of day it was or whether she was disturbing him, simply ringing him when it suited her.

He picked up the phone one morning at eight, believing she would be too tied up at the bakery to call then, so he would be safe. His heart gave an involuntary lurch as he heard her voice.

'Gabe, anyone would think you've been trying to avoid me. Either that or you should sack your secretary. I've left getting on for half a dozen messages for you.'

He covered the receiver with his hand and took a deep breath. 'Yeah, yeah.' He made a huge effort to sound normal. 'I'm sorry. I've been wrapped up in a case, some major hitches, been in constant meetings. I *have* meant to ring.' Plausible vague lies, exactly what the situation needed. It seemed to work because she didn't appear to have heard him, instead sweeping on with her own stream of consciousness in her usual impatient way.

'Well, never mind. I've got hold of you now. It's Ed!' She couldn't keep the excitement out of her voice.

'What about Ed?' *Walked out? Decided to become a monk? Sadly no.*

'The clothes are working! He noticed my new heels right away.'

He grinned ruefully into the phone. 'Told you.'

'And I keep catching him stealing sneaky glances at me when he thinks I'm not looking. He's much more touchy-feely than usual, too. You're a genius! I should market you to women everywhere!'

Gabe felt a stabbing pain somewhere deep in his gut, not unlike a punch. Miserably he realised this was what jealousy must feel like. It wasn't an emotion he was used to. The women he dated never evoked enough interest for him to be bothered if another man came along. His mind spun. It wasn't just a blip, then. Something he could talk himself out of by using willpower. There really had been a shift in his feelings for her. He rubbed his temples with his thumb and forefinger. Problem was, how the hell did he shift them back to where they were supposed to be? Because it was obvious that Lucy didn't feel the same way. And why should she? He was just good old Gabriel, brother-figure, who was currently masterminding her happy ever after with another guy and who'd apparently just kick-started her relationship.

Wanting to get the conversation over with as quickly as he could, he was uncharacteristically abrupt with her. 'Lucy, I've really got to be somewhere, so can we do this later?'

'I'm sorry! I always forget how busy you are. I think of you as my personal property.'

He felt a surge of happiness at this remark followed swiftly by despair. What the hell was he going to do?

'I just wanted to organise getting together,' she said. 'You know, to talk through my proposal. I've got loads of ideas. Maybe we could make it a lunchtime, though, because Ed's been talking about taking me out to dinner.'

What, every night? he wanted to snarl at her. He shook his head briefly to try and clear it. 'Are you sure you really need me, Lucy? I mean, you sound like you're doing great on your own.'

'Of course I need you.' She sounded puzzled

and hurt and he experienced a jolt of guilt. 'I need your views, Gabe. You've helped loads already. I know I haven't been exactly positive about some of your observations, but you know that's just my way. I've taken everything you've said on board.' Then she added cynically, 'Or are you just too busy for friends? Is that it?'

He pulled himself together with a stupendous effort. He was used to his emotions being pretty constant, not this swinging between jealousy, anger and misery. If love was this much grief, he decided he had been thoroughly justified in choosing to give it a miss all this time.

'Don't be silly,' he said, as lightly as he could. 'Like I said, it's just been busy.' He realised he couldn't avoid seeing her. His only hope was to carry on as normal and hope these feelings would just wear off. In fact seeing her might help. Maybe he was building the whole thing up in his mind. 'How about tomorrow?' he suggested. 'I'll meet you at Smith's for a sandwich.'

'Great. Can you make it about two?'

He gritted his teeth in exasperation. 'Do

you always have to eat so late? Can't you have lunch at twelve or one like normal people?'

'I can't help it,' she countered. 'Twelve until one is our busiest time at the shop. We need more than one person to make it run properly. If we make it two, I can leave Sophie in charge and not have to rush back.'

'OK, OK, two it is.' There was no point arguing with her.

He replaced the receiver with a feeling of trepidation.

Lucy put the phone down feeling reassured. Her feelings were focused exactly where they should be. It was just a simple matter of keeping your mind in the right place. She'd made a stand to herself by telling Gabriel in no uncertain terms how wonderfully her relationship plans were going. After all, she reasoned, if she focused enough on Ed there wouldn't be time for feelings for anyone else to develop, especially stupid feelings for Gabriel, which could never come to anything. Things with Ed really *did* seem to have been boosted. Surely that was a good sign. She could make Ed sit up and take notice after two years and that had to stand them in good stead for the future. She could even look at these irrational feelings for Gabriel as a test of her love for Ed. If she could get over this then nothing could shake them once they were committed.

She ignored the small voice inside that told her she was just scared of change. Understandable really after the shifting sand of her childhood. Scared of losing Ed and the secure life she'd built with them both in it, where she knew when she went to sleep what would happen when she woke up again. If she wasn't deliriously in love with him, she certainly loved him for the life and stability they had together. Her mother had loved her father with desperate passion and look where it had got her. No, she was certain. Love that lasted was built on a lot more than lust. And she needed Gabriel as a friend to talk to and lean on in times of trouble. *Mess with that, Lucy,* the voice said, *and everything teeters on the precipice. Follow these mad feelings and end up losing Ed, and then after three weeks, or maybe a month if you're lucky, commitment phobic Gabe will be just about ready to quit, and you can lose him, too.* Because it would never be the same between her and Gabriel again—that was the one thing she knew beyond question. That kind of elephant never left the room.

Plus the fact, she reassured herself, Gabe showed no more sign of reciprocating her feelings now than he had when he was eighteen, so she would most likely make a fool of herself as well. He obviously hadn't given her a second thought this week—she'd had to practically stalk him to get a phone conversation. The best way to put this whole mess behind her would be to direct all her energy at Ed, who she knew loved her and wanted to be with her and who was showing loads more enthusiasm for their relationship than he had in months. She should be making the most of that. Once he'd said yes and they were engaged, everything would be fine, she was sure of it.

It was a perfect winter's day as she walked through the streets from her shop to meet Gabriel at Smith's. This was a quaint little coffee shop in one of the side streets just off the main city centre. She and Gabriel met there often because it was roughly halfway between his office and her shop. The cakes and pastries were always delicious, and Lucy always enjoyed comparing them to those she made in her own bakery. She always judged coffee shops and restaurants by their food; she couldn't seem to stop herself. A dry Danish pastry or a soggy eclair had the instant ability to turn her off an establishment for good. The sun was shining as she walked and the air was crisp and clear. It reminded Lucy of the last day like that, when she'd had lunch at Gabriel's parents' house. She thought of them fondly. Any nostalgia she might have about her childhood had them and their home wrapped up in it.

She wondered sometimes how much further and how much more she might have achieved in life if she'd had an upbringing that hadn't demanded she dive headlong into adult responsibility while she was still in reality just a child. But then on the other hand she was so proud of how far she had come. The fact she'd done it in spite of all that her parents had thrown at her made her achievements all the sweeter.

She allowed herself to think of her parents for a moment. She'd found them creeping into her thoughts more and more frequently these past few days. They had never married, despite the fact it was still really the done thing when she was a child. When things were good and they were getting on sometimes they would talk about it. She remembered her mother even looking at booking the ceremony once and she had been beside herself with excitement. But it never came to anything. It was just forgotten about, never mentioned again. All her schoolfriends had married parents and she had longed to be the same as them. In her child's mind she had built it up to be the answer to all their problems. If only her parents were married they would get along properly and be happy. The fights would stop. Of course as an adult now she knew that wasn't the way things worked. But she still saw marriage as a magical, wonderful thing, a way of cementing a stable relationship. In her mind she knew this wasn't rational, but all the same she had always known she wanted to be married and have a family of her own one day.

She checked her watch and grinned to herself. Late again. Luckily for her she knew Gabriel well enough by now to simply factor in his lousy timekeeping. She didn't expect him for half an hour after the time agreed. As it was, today he arrived only twenty minutes late, looking tired and a little harassed, she thought, but impeccably dressed as ever in a beautifully cut dark blue suit that made his grey-blue eyes seem more intense than ever. He pulled up a chair next to her.

'Do you want anything to eat?' She picked up the menu and scanned it.

He shook his head. 'I've already eaten, like the rest of the human race. Lunchtime for me was an hour and a half ago.' She wasn't used to him being short with her and she looked at him, puzzled. Had she done something to upset him? As she looked he checked his watch.

'Are you in a rush, Gabe?'

He looked up at her distractedly. 'No, why?'

'No reason,' she said, with a hint of irritation. 'Except that you've only just arrived for our lunch date, but you aren't actually planning to eat anything and now you're acting like you need to leave again.'

As she watched him he seemed to shake himself out of his mood and he smiled at her apologetically. 'Sorry. It's been a bit of a manic week.'

She smiled a little. 'It's OK. You don't seem yourself at the moment. I guess this case is taking it out of you.'

He nodded and that feeling of confusion increased. Her conversations with Gabe were never normally stilted like this. Their usual affectionate bickering was a world away from this distracted style of talking. They were interrupted by the waitress, who took their order, Gabriel pointedly asking only for coffee as she defiantly chose a sandwich with side salad. Silence ensued again when the girl left.

'Right, then,' she said, a little uncertainly, when he didn't speak. 'Let me tell you my plans for proposing to Ed. I need you to be totally honest. Don't spare my feelings.'

He gave an odd little half-smile. 'Are you sure you want my total honesty?'

'Of course.'

'Go on, then.'

He was behaving really strangely. She wondered whether she should just scrap the planned discussion and pester him into talking about whatever was bothering him. After the way he had opened up the other night about Alison, she was tempted to try. But in a public place like this she didn't think he would thank her for digging into his thoughts again. If he didn't want to talk he had a stubborn streak that meant he would first clam up and then get angry. Plus the fact she was determined to keep the whole conversation centred on Ed and lock Gabriel well and truly into the role of supportive friend. She had her own agenda here and the best thing to do was surely press on and not to be diverted.

'OK.' She fished a notebook out of her handbag and ignored his raised eyebrows. Before he had the chance to mock the fact that she had actually put something in writing she began skimming her notes. 'Here's what I'm thinking. Book out our favourite restaurant—you know, the Italian place on the square?'

She glanced up at him. He pulled a dubious face but didn't comment.

'Ask all our best friends to come along and get there before us. You'd be invited of course—I'd need you there as moral support.' She tapped him pointedly on the arm with her pen. 'Then we arrive at the prearranged time.' Her voice got louder as she warmed to her subject and several people in the café glanced over. She ignored them. 'Of course, he'll realise all his mates are there and wonder what's going on, and I'll get down on one knee and ask him to marry me. Then we can all have a big celebratory meal and have a fantastic evening! What do you think? Does that work from a male point of view? I thought including our friends would be a good move.'

As she spoke his facial expression had become more and more sceptical, but she refused to be silenced and rushed on with her usual enthusiasm. Still, by the end of her description she had to admit she'd been hoping for a bit more encouragement than this, and to be honest it was taking the wind out of her sails a bit.

'OK, you said you wanted me to be honest and I'll tell you what I think,' he told her. 'Just about everything that could be wrong in that scenario, is.'

She looked at him with barely concealed annoyance. 'Why?'

Gabriel sat back and folded his arms. 'Firstly, inviting all his mates along is the worst thing you could do. Basically what you're doing is embarrassing him. No guy wants to be put on the spot like that. You have to realise you're taking over his role by doing this. Taking over the *male* role. He will for ever be ribbed by his mates about being under the thumb. *Your* thumb, to be specific. Trust me, even if your girlfriend is in charge, you want the world to think that *you* are. It's an unwritten rule.'

There seemed to be a whole book of unwritten rules by which the average man lived, according to Gabriel.

'So go on, then, enlighten me,' she said sarcastically. 'What does your average guy want?'

'Well, he wants to feel like he's the one in charge. He chooses when he makes you his wife and he chooses how he does that.' He leaned in conspiratorially as if imparting a great secret, as if he might suddenly be lynched by a gang of average men if he were overheard handing over this information to the other side. 'You're messing with the natural order of things here, Lucy, and you need to tread carefully.'

She bit her tongue as the waitress appeared with their order. As soon as they were alone again she leaned in towards him. 'The natural order of things? I'm talking about proposing to my boyfriend, not time travel, for goodness' sake.'

'I just meant you need to do it in such a way as it makes him feel like he's got the upper hand.'

'You mean, make him think it was his idea all along.'

'Exactly.'

'Well, how the hell is that possible when the

words “will you marry me?” are going to be coming out of my mouth and not his?’

‘Your approach needs to be different. Submissive. As if you’re asking him an enormous favour. You could include that in the words you choose. Maybe say something like, “I would be honoured if you would consider being my husband” or “I feel my life is worth nothing without you.”’

Lucy stuck two fingers in her mouth and made vomiting sounds.

Gabriel raised an impatient eyebrow and looked at her as if she were a naughty toddler. ‘A little class would be good,’ he remarked. ‘I don’t suggest you take this attitude with him or all you’ll end up with is a resounding *“no”*.’

She sighed and rubbed the corners of her eyes wearily with a thumb and forefinger. ‘I don’t know, Gabe. I’m not sure I want to be his doormat just to get him to agree to marry me. I was thinking he would be delighted to be asked and see it as a massive compliment, not some challenge to his manhood.’

‘That’s because you’re a woman and that’s how you’d feel if he proposed to you. Men don’t think like you do. How many times do I have to tell you?’

She decided to shift the subject a little. 'OK, well, let's come back to the exact wording of the thing. What about the location? Are you saying it's fine to invite everyone who knows us as long as I portray myself in the subservient role, caveman style, or am I just better off asking him when it's just the two of us?'

'Much as I would be sorry not to witness you playing the role of submissive cavewoman to Ed's captain caveman, you'll have far more chance of success if you ask him on his own. If you invite along those Neanderthal football mates that I met, you'll definitely shoot yourself in the foot. All you'll achieve is to make him feel pushed into a corner. He can't say no to you because a) he can't be seen to be so cruel in public and b) he won't want to scupper what you've set up to be a massive party.'

She shook her head. 'But that's good, isn't it? He will be forced to say yes.'

'But for all the wrong reasons. If you push him into it you are just as likely for him to backpedal the moment the party's over. At best he might resent you for putting him on the spot and that's hardly the best start for a marriage made in heaven, is it?'

She sighed. 'I suppose not.' She sipped her

coffee moodily. 'Give me the perfect scenario, then, Einstein, and I'll try and work with that.'

A frown crossed his face and she saw him rearrange his features to hide it. It was so brief that she almost missed it. She couldn't place what it meant, but then apparently it meant nothing because he carried on as before.

'To maximise your chances of a yes, if you're asking the average man to marry you, you need to look hot as hell and you need to do it somewhere quiet without friends or family present, and last but not least you need to do it before you have sex. Definitely not afterwards.'

Lucy almost choked on her coffee. At the mention of sex from Gabe when she felt so mixed up about him she felt a blush creep up slowly from her neck and fought it with all her might. She took a bite of her sandwich to buy time and steady herself, looking down in the hope that the blush would subside and he wouldn't notice. When she felt able she spoke in what she hoped was her normal voice.

'Just as a matter of interest, why not afterwards?' she ventured. 'I would have thought that was the perfect time to do it. When you're all loved up and everything's wonderful.'

Gabriel patted her hand sympathetically and she felt as if electric shocks raced through her fingers at his touch. The thought struck her abruptly that she wasn't sure she could remember a time when she'd jumped like that at Ed's touch, even when they'd first met. She tried to concentrate hard on the conversation.

'Like I keep saying, Lu, you need to start thinking like a man. Before you've had sex you hold all the cards, you have the power, he'll hang on your every word. Afterwards, if you manage to get him to stay awake, anything you say will seem less important to him than going to sleep. It's basic biology.'

Lucy made a disgusted face. 'You lot are emotionally backward,' she complained.

Gabriel laughed out loud. 'We're just different, that's all. If men thought the same way as women Ed would have asked you to marry him months ago. Don't you think that makes life seem dull?'

'No! I think it makes perfect sense!'

Gabriel looked at his watch again and she felt her temper slip a notch.

'Gabe, what is your problem? You seem to be desperate to avoid me at the moment and it's getting on my nerves. Is it too much to ask for you to focus for half an hour on one conversation with me?'

He didn't quite meet her eyes. 'Just busy, you know,' he said vaguely. 'I need to make a move.' He made as if to stand up, then for some reason he clearly thought better of it and sat back down. He looked flustered and uncomfortable and she was on the brink of asking him why when he leaned in unexpectedly and covered her hand with his. Her heart leapt involuntarily inside her chest and her pulse increased.

'Lucy, I really think you should reconsider all this, you know,' he said urgently. Her mouth felt suddenly as dry as sandpaper. Just what was he going to say?

'What do you mean?' She tried her best to keep her voice calm, although she felt oddly as if she might start shaking at any moment.

'I'm your friend, Lucy. I'm going to be totally honest with you. You might not like it but I can't help that.'

Her heartbeat seemed to be getting louder. She could hear it inside her head.

He looked into her eyes. 'I think you want to get married and settle down because you didn't have a settled childhood. You want to build your own little happy ever after. The fact that you're surrounded by Ed's mates in a social circle all playing happy families makes you want it even more. I can understand that, but I think you need to be sure it's what you really want, for the right reasons.'

She looked at him, puzzled. Whatever she'd expected him to say, it wasn't this. 'What exactly are you suggesting?'

He took a deep breath. 'I think you should talk to your parents.'

The words fell on her like rocks. She stood up before she even knew that was what she was going to do. Her chair fell backwards with a clatter at the force of her movement. *How could he?* How hard it had been to start again without them. After the years she'd spent cutting them painfully out of her life. Managing by herself. And he'd been there through all that. All the times he'd backed her up, given her strength in her conviction that it was the right thing to do, that they would hold her back and drag her back down and that she could make a life for herself, she really could. She was suffused by confusion and cold anger.

She wiped her lips with a trembling hand. 'I can't believe you are suggesting I actually talk to them about this. My mother the three-times-wed, most irresponsible, self-centred woman in the universe. My father the lush. Just what the hell makes you think either of them is qualified to advise me on how to successfully live my life?'

'I'm not saying they are. It just seems to me you're so hung up on this dream of two-point-four kids and a dog that you're losing sight of the fact that that doesn't automatically make you happy. This is because of your parents—any amateur psychologist could see that.'

'Even if it is, why is that so wrong? With a childhood like mine I certainly know what I'm *not* going to do and that's pretty much everything they did!' Her temper was completely out of control now and she was distantly aware that she was shouting.

Gabriel kept his voice calm and soothing, but to her it just sounded patronising. 'Lu, you had no security as a kid. That's why you're craving it now.' He opened his mouth to continue but she cut him off.

'You've obviously taken temporary leave of your senses,' she snapped. She snatched her bag from the floor and then rounded on him. 'I asked for your help, Gabriel. Your *help.* All I wanted was some pointers on what might make a guy tick, some ideas on how I might propose in a fun way that Ed would like. I didn't ask for a critique of my life as I know it and I certainly didn't expect the suggestion that I undo all the changes I've made for the better. After everything they put me through. And everything I've done to put it right. You're meant to be my friend. Some friend!'

'Lucy…' His voice was shocked but she ignored it and turned to walk towards the door, leaving him standing at the table looking after her. 'Lucy, wait!'

She turned back towards him, oblivious to the interested stares from the other customers and the silence that had fallen as they turned to watch and listen. 'Just stay away from me!'

The door slammed behind her as she stormed from the café.

CHAPTER SIX

LUCY ignored the ringing telephone and took another batch of cupcakes out of the oven. The little kitchen in her flat was filled with the sweet smell of baking and cooking utensils were balanced on every available surface. Her hair was in an untidy bun on top of her head and the front of her T-shirt was dusted with flour because she couldn't be bothered to put on an apron. A couple of hours since her argument with Gabriel and at last she felt calm and focused. Cooking always did that for her. If she ever needed to think something over she gravitated to the kitchen. A lucky side-effect of her anger seemed to be heightened creativity. Some of her best cake creations had resulted from the most stressful moments in her life.

She glanced up as her mobile phone beeped and vibrated loudly on the counter with a text message, and she leaned across to turn it off with a jam-covered finger. She didn't even need to look at it to know it was Gabriel. He had never been able to stand it for long when they had an argument. She, on the other hand, preferred to keep her distance until she calmed down, and depending on the subject of the argument that could be anything from a few hours to a few days.

What he'd said about her parents had really touched a nerve. Her denial that they had anything to do with her desire to settle down was genuine. After all, she hadn't really interacted with either of them for years now. It hurt, too, that this had come from Gabriel, on whom she had always relied for justification of her actions.

She dripped red food colouring into a bowl of white icing and began to beat it with a wooden spoon. It streaked a lovely shade of pink. She wasn't an idiot. She'd always known she wanted a proper settled family one day. Her childhood had been so difficult it would be some kind of miracle if it hadn't shaped the person she was now. It wasn't so much this that bothered her as Gabriel's implication that what had happened years ago was the *only* reason for a decision she was making now. That getting married was the wrong thing for her to do but that she was incapable of seeing it. Why would he say that? Why was he being so horrible, seeming to try everything in his power to put her off the idea?

She began to deftly spread the icing over some heart-shaped shortbreads. Her childhood did affect her decision because it had contributed to who she was. But the reasons she wanted to get married now were present-day reasons, not past ones. Her age, for example. She knew she wanted children and she was nearly thirty. She wanted to get started on that sooner, not later, and she also knew she wanted to be married beforehand. Her work, her financial security—the business had really gained a foothold now; it was doing exceptionally well, far exceeding her expectations. And of course her relationship. She had been happy with Ed for a good length of time now. She knew his bad habits and she knew she could live with them. He wasn't Mr Perfect, but she honestly believed he was Mr Perfect For Her. He was fundamentally a good man, he was good to her and, very importantly, he supported her business ambitions wholeheartedly, even when she was having success and he was putting up with setbacks. She was just ready to take the next step; it was that simple.

But do you love him, Lucy? Really love him? Yes, she told herself, firmly. That wasn't up for debate. She squashed the nagging little voice that reminded her she didn't feel the same depth of passion for Ed as she once had for Gabriel. She was just a kid back then. She knew now there were different kinds of love, and the kind she needed for the life she wanted was the reliable, constant kind, wasn't it? She refused to let her mind explore what alternative to that there might be.

Yet however hard she tried to stop it her mind kept slipping back to what Gabriel had said. She was unable to brush it aside, put it out of her mind. She worried at it, picked at it. She liked to think she was fully in control of her life now. She was in the driving seat, no one else. *If that's true, then why not talk to your parents and test it?* The idea made her heart beat faster and her palms feel clammy, classic signs of nervousness. Slamming the empty icing bowl into the already-full sink, she finally made the decision that had been lurking at the back of her mind for hours now. The only way to prove to herself that she was really and truly her own person, to prove Gabriel wrong, was to talk to one of them. It would have to be her father, she supposed. She had no idea where her mother was except that it was somewhere in Las Vegas. She had her father's address stashed somewhere and Birmingham was only a few hours away. There was nothing else for it if she was to put the niggling doubts Gabriel had planted behind her.

Gabriel made himself put the telephone down. He'd left three messages now and had sent a couple of texts. She would speak to him when she was ready. She always did. But he couldn't shake the nagging feeling that he'd gone too far this time. He'd gone to meet her intent on encouraging her to follow her plans to settle down with Ed. To play the supportive best friend, just as he always did. Certainly not to betray his true feelings for her. But watching her talking about how she could do her best to persuade another guy to marry her had gradually, minute by minute, become unbearable. Ed took her for granted and patently didn't deserve her. If he did he would have married her ages ago.

Gabriel sighed miserably. He'd lost control.

There was no other way to describe it. He'd wanted to try and talk her out of it, question her love for Ed, persuade her she was making a mistake, but he hadn't quite dared. He was too afraid of what she might say, that it would be something he didn't want to hear. And so instead he'd hit her below the belt. He had mentioned her parents for no other reason than to selfishly put a damp cloth over her excitement at the prospect of proposing. In doing so he hadn't considered for a second how she might feel about him throwing her family into the mix. He could kick himself. He'd been there throughout her childhood. He'd dried her tears when she'd run to the manor house to escape the rows. He'd dressed the cuts on her hand that time when she'd hurt herself cleaning up a broken bottle after one of the more physical arguments. She'd been just a kid at the time. What the hell had he been thinking dragging all that back up for her again?

He desperately wanted to go to her and apologise, make things right. But knowing her as well as he did, he knew there was no point trying to force her to talk until she was ready. He had to go to an important client meeting but he found it impossible to follow properly what was said. His mind was consumed by Lucy.

'Would you mind waiting? I won't be long.' Lucy leaned forward and spoke to the taxi driver before climbing out of the cab. She surveyed the house on the opposite side of the street. A tiny nondescript terrace in a nondescript street. She briefly checked the slip of paper in her hand. This was it; this was the place. His place. Her palms felt hot and clammy and she unconsciously rubbed them slowly against her coat as she walked towards the grimy front door. To knock or not to knock, that was the question.

Before she could back out, she raised her knuckles and knocked. Then knocked again, loudly.

He isn't home. Let's just get back to Bath, Lucy. Bad idea.

She banged this time with her fist and, bending to open the letterbox, called out, 'Dad!' for good measure. She could see through it into a dingy-looking hall with a brown carpet.

At last a shuffling sound could be heard and a shadow loomed behind the frosted glass of the front door. She caught her breath as the latch rattled and then as the door swung open her heart began hammering in her chest. And there he was. Old now and grey, with a few days' scruffy growth of white stubble and unkempt clothes. Her father. Not quite what she'd prepared herself for. In her mind she'd built him up to be some kind of monster, but this was the reality. A pitiful, scruffy old man. A stale smell drifted from the hallway behind him.

'Lucinda,' he said in obvious surprise. 'Well, well, well. What are you doing here?'

No endearments. No 'pleased to see you'. Just an indifferent tone. Had she really expected anything else?

'I was in the area,' she said lamely. 'Work… you know. I'm on my way back to the station. I thought I'd drop by and see how you are.'

The eyes looking at her from the heavily lined face were shrewd. 'Ten years long gone, and in all that time nothing more than a card or phone call.'

Lucy looked away with a jolt of embarrassment, and was immediately angry with herself for doing so. What did he expect after the way he'd treated her? By the time she'd finally left he was drunk every night. He'd rarely spoken to her except to hurl insults and she'd been cleaning, cooking, shopping, trying to hold things together. She'd tried to make him get help with his drinking but he'd been sinking in his own self-pity since her mother had left and he had no inclination to find a way out.

Then she'd got a place at catering college. A means of escape. And once she'd left she'd simply kept running, that was all. Instead of going back home when her course finished, she'd rented a tiny flat in Swindon because it was cheap. Working for a pittance in a local restaurant to build up her experience, she'd spent every spare minute baking cakes and had built up a steady bank of customers in the local area who came to her for wedding and celebration cakes. After Swindon, she'd stayed with Gabriel in Bath before getting her own place and starting her business. It hadn't been a difficult decision to not return to Gloucestershire. Staying away had always been the better choice than going home. Oh, she'd kept in touch of course, but only the bare minimum. A phone call now and then, cards occasionally. Any guilt she might have felt at leaving was assuaged by the fact her father had never once made any proper attempt to contact her himself and make things right. He'd let her know when he'd changed address but he never bothered with birthday or Christmas cards. She'd sometimes wondered if the change of address notices were so the authorities would know who to notify when he eventually drank himself to death. The gap between them had grown over the years until now here they stood, virtual strangers.

'Must be a reason for you to visit,' he said. 'All this time. Why now?'

He could still read her like an open book, she realised. She'd never been able to keep secrets from him. Goosebumps prickled on her arms. He made no move to invite her in and she was glad.

'I'm thinking of getting married,' she blurted out suddenly, before she even knew what she was going to say.

He nodded slowly, holding her gaze the entire time with the sharp eyes, green just like her own, and a sarcastic grin spread across his face. 'You want my blessing?' He gave a dry chuckle.

She took a nervous step backwards. 'No,' she said. 'I don't need your blessing. I just…' She paused and looked at him closely. The grin was gone. The face was lined and old; tiny broken vessels from the heavy drinking reddened his nose and cheeks. The man was a shell of the person he once was. She realised her overwhelming feeling at that moment was pity for him. He certainly couldn't hurt her or scare her any more. 'I just thought you should know,' she finished.

His face softened almost imperceptibly and he nodded. 'I'm pleased for you.' His voice sounded gruff and he rummaged in his shirt pocket with his fingers. Removing his cigarettes, he lit one and, leaning against the door jamb, squinted at her through the smoke. 'What's he like, then, our Lucinda? Is he good enough for you?'

She felt the back of her throat tingle suddenly and tears pricked at her eyes. Despite all that had happened he was still her father. And however he felt about her, however many years had gone by, he'd cared enough to ask. She swallowed hard to make the tears go away.

'Yes, Dad, he's a good man. He makes me happy,' she managed.

He drew hard on his cigarette and nodded firmly. 'You hang onto him, then. Tell him your old man says he'd better look out for you.'

She smiled suddenly at him and a smile touched his lips in return. She was glad she'd come after all. For the first time she felt she had control over a conversation with him. What could he say or do now that would hurt her? She was an adult now, not a scared kid any more. She had her own life, with no need of him in it. The balance of power had shifted while she'd been away and she could choose the terms on which she let him back in, if she did at all.

'How are you, Dad?' she ventured, more confidently. 'How's work?'

'I get by.' He shifted a little awkwardly. 'I'd invite you in, but I only rent a room here. It's difficult…'

She didn't mind. A few minutes was quite enough for today anyway. She had plenty to think about. It had been a big enough step just coming here and speaking to him.

'Maybe next time. I have to get a move on anyway.' She nodded towards the taxi waiting on the opposite side of the road. 'It's only a flying visit.'

He sighed and nodded. 'It's good to see you, Lucinda.' The green eyes were serious this time and she held his gaze. He seemed weaker, somehow. Smaller. The terrifying presence she remembered so vividly from her childhood was gone.

'You, too, Dad. I'll be in touch.' She smiled at him one more time and then made a move towards the taxi. Halfway across the road he called to her and she turned back.

'You couldn't lend me some money, could you, love?'

Exasperated, she walked back towards him, rummaging in her bag for her purse. And it was then that it dawned on her that he hadn't really changed at all. He hadn't moved on. She had.

Gabriel parked the Aston Martin in the square opposite Lucy's bakery and got out. Darkness was falling quickly and the streetlamps were already on, casting a golden glow. Standing hesitantly by the car, he questioned himself for a moment. So she hadn't rung him back since they'd argued—so what? But then when he'd eventually become impatient enough to call Ed, he'd mentioned in passing that she'd gone to Birmingham to visit someone. That had rung alarm bells with Gabriel, although he was initially unable to put his finger on the reason why. Then eventually it had come to him.

Lucy at the dinner table with his parents. 'My father's in Birmingham. A friend offered him a job...'

How well he knew her. Almost well enough to have a stab at reading her thoughts? Perhaps she was still just angry with him and wanted space. Or perhaps she'd been to see her father.

Locking the car, he strode decisively across the square. The shop, with its sign 'Have Your Cake…' depicted retro style in icing-sugar pink on a pistachio green backdrop, was closed, just as he would have expected at this time of day. But he knew her better than anyone.

A couple of passers-by glanced curiously at the tall man pressing his hands against the cold glass of the cake shop window. Gabriel was oblivious to them. Shading his eyes, he could see nothing but the faint outline of the empty display cabinets and the counter. Then, as his eyes became accustomed to the dark, there at the back he saw a chink of light around the door that led to the back of the premises. To the kitchen, where the big ovens were, and the worktops where the cakes and pastries were made. He was right. She was here.

Feeling triumphant at how well he knew her, he left the shop front and felt his way down the narrow alley at the side to the back entrance, his fingertips trailing along the rough sand-papery bricks as he felt his way along in the semi-darkness. Light streamed from the window at the back of the shop and he saw her rusty old Mini car parked up tightly against the wall.

Trying the door, he was surprised when it opened easily, immediately assaulting his senses with the warm delicious smell of baking. He felt a burst of exasperation that she'd left the door unlocked. How many times had he harped on about personal safety to her?

'Lucy!' he shouted as he walked in, so as not to alarm her. There was no reply, so he continued along the short passageway to the kitchen, and then, rounding the corner, he took a deep breath as he saw her.

Her unruly hair was caught up roughly out of her face with a pencil stuck through it; a smudge of flour crossed her cheek. She was adding drops of a bright green liquid to a huge billowing white mound of something cake-looking on the counter in front of her. Her face was paler than ever, no sign of any colour on the high cheekbones. There were dark smudges beneath her eyes. But he didn't miss the fact that her mouth had a determined set to it.

'Lucy,' he said again, loudly enough that she couldn't fail to hear him. There were batches of cakes and pastries on every surface. God knew how long she'd been here.

'I'm busy.' She didn't even bother to look up, simply whisking the green liquid into the white gloop, watching it streak.

He grimaced involuntarily. 'What the hell is that?'

'A bit like a meringue,' she said, looking at it appraisingly. And then, glancing up at him, 'I'm experimenting with some funky macaroons.'

'Looks like you've liquidised a frog.'

A second glance up at him. And the faint glimmer of a smile touched the corners of her mouth. His heart twisted as he noticed how tired she looked. He ached to just grab her and sweep her into a hug and he clenched his fists in a supreme effort to stop himself doing just that. He needed to talk to her first. To apologise. To make it right.

'Lucy, I'm sorry,' he said. When she didn't look up, he walked over to her. Putting an arm around her, he firmly removed the spatula from her hand and cast it onto the worktop next to the ghastly blob of green stuff. She still didn't speak but she made no move to stop him as he propelled her over to a chair. Pushing her to sit down, he knelt down in front of her and took both of her cold hands in his. They were sticky from the cake mixture.

He looked deeply into her clear green eyes. 'I had no right to talk to you like that about your parents.' He searched her face for some response. 'After everything they put you through, I don't know what I was thinking.' She simply looked at him as he squeezed her hands. 'Lucy, I'm so sorry.'

'How did you know I'd be here?' she asked, after a moment.

He smiled gently at her. 'Because I know *you,* Lu. Almost as well as you know yourself. Remember when there was that hitch when you were setting up the shop lease? And that time you crashed your car? You trashed my kitchen and cooked for England. When normal people need time to think they go for a drive, or maybe a walk. You cook. You had to be somewhere with an oven. I tried your flat. I just narrowed it down.'

A wry smile.

'So am I forgiven?' He looked at her hopefully.

She smiled at him properly this time and he felt a surge of relief that made his head swim.

'You are forgiven,' she said. 'But only on condition that you quit stepping outside your remit. I asked you for a few pointers on how to propose. I didn't expect you to try and counsel me about my past like some agony aunt. Agreed?'

He could hear the tiredness in her voice but she sounded absolutely resolute. He was prepared to accept anything at this moment in order to make it all right.

'Agreed,' he said, thankfully. Standing up, he hooked another chair from the corner of the room with one foot and pulled it over, sitting down next to her.

She loosened her unruly curls and caught them back up, forcing the pencil more securely through them. 'Anyway, things didn't turn out so badly after all,' she told him, without meeting his eyes. 'I took your advice and went to see my dad.' And without waiting for any further response from him she stood up and went back to the worktop, picking up the spatula and scooping a blob of the green macaroon mixture onto some baking paper.

'Oh?' He didn't dare venture any comment for fear of saying the wrong thing. She'd only just forgiven his behaviour and there was no way he intended to risk another argument.

She glanced briefly around at him. 'I know,' she said. 'I can't believe it, either. I'm really proud of myself. I was so angry with you for suggesting I let them back into my life. You had no right. But the trouble was, once you'd said it I couldn't stop thinking about it. It drove me mad, until I just had to go and see him to find out how I really feel.'

'And how do you really feel?' He wasn't sure he really wanted to know the answer to that.

'Well, I'm not scared of him any more.' She put the spatula down and turned to face him, leaning back against the worktop. 'You should see him, Gabe. He's just a sad old man now. His drinking doesn't look any better but he seems to be holding down a job, so it can't be that terrible, can it? I feel like maybe I could have a relationship with him now on my own terms. I have my own life now and I can choose how much of a part he plays in that. I'm totally in control.' She smiled at him and his heart felt as if it would liquefy at the relief he saw in her face. 'It's a good feeling. I've been putting him out of my mind for so long. It's so lovely not to have to do that any more.'

It was no good. He had to ask the question that bothered him the most. 'And how's things with Ed?' He kept his voice as neutral as he could, betraying no feelings.

The oven alarm sounded suddenly and they both jumped. Lucy broke their eye contact to cross the room and remove some cupcakes. With her back to him she was mercifully unable to see the agony that crossed Gabriel's face as she said, 'Good, thanks. If anything this has made me more certain than ever.' She put the cakes down on a cooling rack and turned back to him, removing the oven gloves from her hands.

'Really? You're going ahead with the proposal?' His heart felt like lead in his chest. As if someone had wrung it suddenly, or maybe stamped on it.

'Yes.' She took a skewer from the counter and stabbed it into one of the cupcakes. 'You've done me a favour, Gabe. If I wasn't sure before I damn well am now. I can't change my past but I *can* shape my future. What I have with Ed is based on the most important things. All the things that were missing for my parents, why their relationship was such a train wreck. Ed and I don't compare with what they were. I can make my own family now and I know I'll get it right.'

Gabriel's heart constricted in his chest. He forced himself to smile at her. 'Great. That's great. I'm sure it will all be fine.'

She looked really happy. Tired but determined. And she'd been through so much. He dug his nails into his palms so hard that they left a mark. *Because of your selfish desire to keep her to yourself you've put her through hell this last week. Well, no more.* As he stood there in that moment he hated himself more than he'd ever hated anyone. He, who was supposed to care about her, not caring how much he hurt her as long as the outcome was what he wanted. He now admitted to himself that he loved her. That he'd loved her for years. It was pointless denying it. Too late to tell her now and it served him right. How could he turn her life upside down again when she was so happy and settled?

He made a decision on the spot. He would back right off. And with good grace this time.

No petulant outbursts like the one he'd had in Smith's. She would get married to Ed. Live a long and happy life with her kids and her business. And he would stick with the role of friend. Embrace it and be grateful for it. This week he'd proved to himself that he was barely worthy of that.

She was moving the cupcakes onto a rack now, her attention totally taken up with them. He needed to get out of here.

'I'll get going now, Lu. I can see you're busy.' He walked steadily across the room and leaned over her shoulder to kiss her cheek. Closing his eyes, he breathed in the scent of her. She smelled sweet, like vanilla, and he felt his body respond instantly, involuntarily. He clenched his fists tightly and stepped away immediately as if burned. She was so engrossed in what she was doing that she didn't even notice.

'OK,' she said without looking up. 'I'll see you tomorrow, then. What time are you picking me up?'

He floundered momentarily. What the hell was she talking about? And then he remembered. His work dinner. That would be some kind of torture now. But maybe he could use it as an opportunity to work on their friendship. Set some new boundaries that might help him to let go of the image of her as something more than a friend. As his lover. Find a way to help him carry on as just her friend.

'I'll pick you up at seven,' he called over his shoulder on the way out. He didn't wait for an answer.

CHAPTER SEVEN

LUCY looked appraisingly at her reflection in the mirror. She couldn't remember the last time she'd worn a cocktail dress. College ball, maybe? Even then she didn't think she'd ever worn anything as lovely as this. Following the success of the personal shopping session, she'd picked a dress outside the scope of what she would normally wear. It was a simple sheath of black silk, ankle length and bias cut so it skimmed her body in all the right places, giving the impression of curves for once despite the fact she hardly had any. The spaghetti straps showed off the creamy skin of her shoulders and the back was daringly low cut. She had bought a soft black wrap to go with it. The whole outfit had cost more than she could remember spending on one shopping trip, ever. But she'd done her best to ignore her frugal instincts. Gabriel would be proud of her progress, she thought. With a lot of work and plenty of hair products she'd even managed to tame her curls for once. She'd pinned the front sections back and the bulk of her hair cascaded over her bare shoulders and down her back. A few tendrils escaped, framing her face.

A normal night out for her was a meal down at the local pub with Ed, for which she barely made the effort to wash the flour out of her hair. She sprayed perfume in a cloud and walked into it, the way the magazines said you should. She had to admit that she was enjoying the evening so far. It was lovely to get dressed up for a change.

She wouldn't let herself think about Gabriel in any other way than as a friend. That had all been some minor head rush, cold feet about settling down, nothing more. The argument about her parents had made it easier to ignore those feelings; she had been so angry with him. She refused to think about the way her heart had raced at the bakery yesterday when Gabriel had apologised and had looked into her eyes and held her hands. Furious anger with him followed by the misplaced heart-thumping desire that she'd spent the last days fighting. Two extremes.

Does Ed ever make you feel that intense? her mind whispered suddenly, and she suppressed the thought. Tonight would be a good opportunity to get her friendship with Gabriel back on track after their argument. And then tomorrow night she was going to take her life in her hands and propose to Ed. It was all going to turn out perfectly. She closed her eyes briefly. So why did she feel more excited, more on edge, more *alive* about tonight than she did about tomorrow?

She stepped into the black high heels. Instantly the hang of the dress was perfected and the girl in the mirror had a proper womanly figure for a change instead of her usual look of an orphan who could do with feeding up. A dab of lip gloss and she was ready. She checked the clock. It was almost seven. She decided to wait through Gabriel's customary late half-hour downstairs. She could put the TV on and take her mind off her nerves bubbling in her stomach.

For once she actually thought he had outdone himself. Just five minutes had passed before the buzzer sounded, and she pressed the button to open the door and then returned to the sitting room to search for her handbag. She heard the door slam and then footsteps entered the room. She dropped lip gloss and keys into her bag without looking up.

'Pretty much on time—makes a change,' she joked, and then turned around with a grin to see not Gabriel, but Ed, dressed in jeans and a T-shirt.

He let out a low whistle. 'Wow.'

She smiled at him uncertainly. 'I wasn't expecting you.'

'I know. I just thought I'd pop in on the way to the pub.' He was looking at her as if he'd never seen her before.

'Do I look OK?' She turned this way and that, trying to appraise the hang of the dress. She felt a little shy, even with Ed, simply because it was so far removed from anything she normally wore. The heels were three inches, so for once she almost matched Ed for height. Gabe was taller than Ed and so would still tower above her, of course, but she was used to that.

'You look stunning,' he said. 'Shame it's going to be wasted on Gabriel.' He looked her up and down. 'Still…' he walked over to her and ran a finger down her bare back '…I could make up for it now.'

She wriggled away before she could think about how that would look. 'Not now, Ed. It's taken for ever to make my hair look like something other than a bird's nest. The last thing I need is to roll around on the sofa.'

Ed retreated across the room as if stung, and guilt stabbed at her as she caught his hurt expression.

'I'm sorry,' she gabbled. 'I'm just nervous, I suppose. Not used to parties like this, and I won't know anyone apart from Gabe.' She gave a little laugh and walked back towards him, intending to compensate for giving him the brush off. But Ed was having none of it.

He pushed her away roughly as she tried to put her arms around his neck. 'If I didn't know better I'd think there was something going on between the two of you. First you start dressing differently and spending more time with him, and now you're done up like a dog's dinner as his escort and you give me the cold shoulder. When the hell do you dress like this for me? That's what I'd like to know.'

Not this, not now. Jittery enough already at the prospect of the evening ahead, she had to take deep breaths to keep herself calm.

'You're not being fair,' she protested. 'Yes,

I've changed my clothes a bit, but only because I thought I was looking a bit tired and boring. And you've got a cheek criticising me for seeing Gabe. You've been out with your mates four times this week.' She turned on her heel and left the room, angry and upset. She hated arguments like this. It transported her back to her childhood when she used to sit on the top stair and listen to the raised voices below. She tried her best to always solve problems calmly, whoever she was talking to, but she had to admit that sometimes she didn't find it easy. She had quite a quick temper and it didn't always behave the way she would have liked it to.

'There's an important distinction though, Lucy,' he shouted after her. 'My mates are all men!'

He stormed after her and caught up with her in the kitchen. 'What would you think if I took a woman out for the evening to a work party? I think I've been more than understanding under the circumstances.' He pointed an emphatic finger at her as she turned to face him. 'In fact I think I've been an absolute saint. And it's gone on long enough. You're not going tonight. I forbid it. So you might as well go and get that dress off and put some jeans on.' He had the air of someone who expected his bidding to be done without question.

Lucy felt any control she retained over her anger disappear and she let fly with full force. 'Don't you dare tell me what to do! This has nothing to do with me having a relationship with Gabe. I'm doing a favour for a friend and that's all. It has *everything* to do with your lazy approach to everything about you and me. When do I dress like this for you? When the hell do you take me anywhere that has a dress code other than jeans?' She opened her clutch bag and pawed through its contents in search of her house keys. She would find them and wait outside. Gabriel would be picking her up at any moment and she didn't want him to wander inadvertently into World War Three. Ed could let himself out.

She found the keys as he snarled his answer.

'If you weren't so damn tired from working God-knows-what hours then maybe we'd have a bit more of a social life. But you're the one who can't leave that damn bakery alone for five minutes. And when I ask you to show a bit of interest in *my* business, put some investment my way, there's zero interest. Zilch.'

A horn sounded outside. She couldn't have timed it better herself. Maybe she and Gabe had some psychic link that enabled him to read her mind.

'I can't do this now,' she said. 'I'm going out.' She walked carefully down the hall towards the front door, deliberately placing one foot in front of the other in the unfamiliar high heels. They clicked against the wooden floor.

'Get back here. You're not going anywhere!'

She ignored Ed's shout but as she slammed the door behind her she couldn't stop the tears beginning to burn at the back of her throat. The night was cloudy and she could feel the threat of rain. It perfectly matched the way she felt. She ran without looking back down the steps to the silver Aston Martin and climbed in. Only then did she look back. Only then did she realise that she'd absolutely expected Ed to run after her out of the house. The door remained closed. He hadn't bothered. She wondered for a moment how she felt about that, what it might say about Ed's feelings for her. She didn't like the thought that right now they seemed to be growing apart instead of closer.

'Are you OK?' Gabriel looked like James Bond in his perfectly cut dinner suit. His eyes looked deeper blue-grey than ever against the black jacket combined with his dark hair. His face was full of nothing but concern for her.

'Just drive,' she said. She pulled the visor down in front of her so she could use the mirror. Fishing in her clutch bag for a tissue, she used a corner of it to carefully mop her eyes without smearing the eye make-up that had taken the best part of half an hour to get right. All these small deliberate movements helped her to get her temper back under control. Gabriel did exactly as she asked and as the car purred smoothly away he didn't speak to her for several minutes. Some unobtrusive and soothing classical music drifted from the car stereo. She found herself marvelling at the way he knew exactly the behaviour she needed from him. Not a huge inquest into whether she was OK or not, or twenty questions about why she was upset. Just a calm background, which allowed her to gather her thoughts and fight the tears back into submission. Again she found him instinctively knowing how to act with her in a way Ed never did.

She used the peace to gather her thoughts about Ed. There was a part of her that was a tiny bit pleased by his angry possessiveness,

Neanderthal as it was. The idea that she'd been able to make a few changes and make him take stock of what he had. If nothing else his jealousy, the fact he was so aware of the change in her appearance, showed that his regard for her was clear. She watched Gabriel wistfully, fighting the pang of regret that she had never been able to provoke such a reaction in him. He hadn't even bothered to stay until the end of her styling session. If only it were Gabe feeling jealous, but he barely seemed to acknowledge that she was female half the time. She felt a rush of shame at how these thoughts betrayed Ed. She wanted things with Ed to work the way they always had, not be thrown into disarray like this.

Only when Gabriel glanced across and could see she was calm did he venture any comment. 'Ed still alive?'

She gave a bitter laugh and he smiled his gorgeous lopsided smile at her. He'd always teased her about her temper when they were kids, describing it as a hurricane, against her indignant protestations.

'How do you know this is about Ed?'

'Well, I think the whole street probably heard you slam that front door,' he said. 'In fact I'm surprised the building is still standing.' When she didn't laugh this time he looked briefly across at her again. 'Are you OK, Lu?' He took his hand from the steering wheel and placed it over hers. She felt a sparkling rush of electricity start in her wrists and spread slowly up her arms. The softness in his voice made the tears threaten again and she swallowed hard. *Keep it together, Lucy.*

'Do you want to talk about it?' he ventured, concern obvious in his voice.

She shook her head vigorously. 'It's just a stupid row.' Her voice sounded thick through her stuffy nose.

Why does my heart leap like this when he touches me? Why him and not Ed? She didn't want this. Her future with Ed meant so much to her and she wanted to feel passion for him, not Gabriel or anyone else. She wished she could force her body to react to Ed in the way it did to Gabriel, tingling at his touch and melting when he looked at her in a certain way, but it seemed mind control only went so far and her body was working to its own subconscious agenda.

Maybe she should drop this whole proposal thing. All this upheaval had only begun when she started planning it all out. Her heart sank miserably at the thought. She'd spent so long wanting her happy family it made her throat tighten to think of giving it up. But she wasn't sure she could ignore the growing feeling that she'd be settling for Ed when he just didn't inspire the passion in her that she knew she felt for Gabriel. Was settling for someone really good enough? For Ed or for her?

'Let's just forget about it and concentrate on tonight,' Gabriel said. 'This isn't a social evening, you know, it's practically a career move. Get this wrong and it could set back my senior partnership prospects by a good few years. It's vital to look and play the part in the right way.'

She shook her head at him, exasperated. 'Don't you think you're taking the whole thing a bit seriously? Surely your bosses wouldn't make a business decision based on who you roll up with at some work function.'

'They might,' he said, glancing across at her. 'Sleeping with work colleagues isn't seen as best practice in current legal circles.'

'Well, why do it, then?'

He shrugged. 'It always seems like a good idea at the time. And it's never meant to be anything serious.'

She was relieved to be talking about him rather than dwelling on her own problems.

'That's where you're going wrong. You obviously don't understand women.' She pointed at him with an emphatic finger. 'If a woman sleeps with you, it's an emotional investment, Gabriel. Most women would follow that up by wondering how your surname would sound after their first name.' She got out her lip gloss and, looking in the visor mirror again, reapplied it before adding, 'And you wonder why they get fed up when you ditch them after a month.'

He grinned. 'Actually I found that a month was a bit long. They tend to be far more accepting if you only see them for three weeks max.'

'You're such a pain.' She looked at him wearily.

'You like me that way, though. You'd hate it if I never annoyed you.' He winked quickly across at her before turning his attention back to the road.

She smiled down at her hands. He was right. His lunacy was just what she needed to cheer her up.

When Gabriel parked the car he opened the

door for her, and when she stood up next to him her new heels meant the difference in their height was much more balanced than it usually was. She was used to feeling tiny next to him but now she only had to tip her chin up slightly to look at him properly. She was sharply aware of his hand resting in the small of her back as they walked towards the entrance. The dinner was being held in an exclusive hotel in the city centre and she couldn't hide a delighted little gasp as they walked through the huge double doors into the ballroom. The room had typically lovely ornate high ceilings, like so many of the beautiful Georgian buildings in Bath. It was dimly lit and large circular tables framed a gleaming parquet dance floor. The tables were set with impeccable white china and linen and silver cutlery twinkled beside crystal wine goblets in the candlelight. A jazz band was playing background music at one end of the room, something mellow with a lot of piano, and later there would be dancing. Lucy couldn't remember having been in a room that looked lovelier.

Gabriel took two flutes of champagne from the silver tray of a passing waiter and handed one to her.

'Thanks.' She took a sip and surveyed the room. The men looked wonderful in dinner dress but it was the women who really caught her attention. There were dresses in every colour imaginable. She looked down at herself briefly, and wished for a moment that she hadn't chosen black. How predictable. Much as she'd loved her dress, it now felt drab.

As if he could read her mind Gabriel leaned in and whispered in her ear, 'You look beautiful, by the way. I didn't get the chance to tell you in the car.' She felt his breath against her neck and it made her feel suddenly light-headed. A warm tingling sensation made its way slowly down her body. Her legs felt unsteady. She took another, larger, sip of the champagne. What on earth would Gabriel think if he knew she was having to mentally squash the thought of what his hands might feel like if he touched her like a lover instead of a friend? Her face felt overly warm and she was glad the room was dark. She hoped it would hide her blushes.

Gabriel was smiling and nodding as they walked through the room. 'Must introduce you to a few people,' he said. Sliding an arm around her waist, he propelled her further into the room. She was more aware of his hand against her than of anything else going on, as if her senses had been realigned. The music passed her by. The people were irrelevant.

Gabriel was quite proud of the way he was holding it together. Even after an hour in her company he still couldn't believe how stunning Lucy looked in the silk dress. The fabric clung to her so that he almost felt he could see the contours of her body through it. And the heels made her legs seem to go on for ever. He was actually grateful for the diversion provided by her argument with Ed, much as he hated seeing her upset. At least it meant she hadn't noticed that he was struggling to keep calm while his heart was thundering in his chest. He'd kept his eyes firmly on the road for the best part of the journey, giving him a chance to get himself under control. *Just friends,* he kept telling himself. Perhaps if he repeated that mantra throughout the evening he would be OK.

Their table turned out to be one of the ones close to the jazz band and Lucy was secretly pleased. It gave her somewhere other to look than at Gabriel. It seemed she couldn't trust her body to behave itself and so she would have to rely on external diversions to get through the evening without making a fool of herself. Gabriel would surely think it hilarious if he knew she was suddenly finding him attractive. She tried hard to keep her mind on Ed. Loyal Ed, who'd always been enough for her before. He was obviously feeling very insecure in their relationship and she hated herself for stirring up feelings like that. In fact he probably had every reason to jump to the wrong conclusion about her and Gabriel after the clothes thing, and the fact Gabriel had been around so much in the last couple of weeks. Everything he'd said to her at her flat had been rooted in the truth.

Really, Lucy? Is it really such a wrong conclusion? She felt cheated that she didn't seem able to get that depth of connection with Ed that she had with Gabe. She would be mad to still consider marriage when she had these doubts. Why press ahead when her head was being turned like this? *Because these feelings for Gabriel aren't real, Lucy. No good can come of them.* Ed was real. In the car Gabriel was just so perfect after Ed's outburst at the flat, knowing exactly how to behave as if he could read her mind. He affected her in so many ways that Ed didn't. But things with Ed were surely too good to throw away on something that could never be. She was so confused.

The evening wore on. The food was delicious. A warm duck salad starter, followed by the most impeccably cooked steak in a delicious sauce. Lucy found she had little appetite, though, and when she looked at Gabriel's plate she could see he'd barely touched his food, too.

As coffee was finally being served people began to disperse around the room after sitting at the tables for the duration of the meal. Lucy felt nervous butterflies rise a little in her stomach. It had been easy while the food was served. Each circular table seated ten people and the conversation had flowed freely between them. There was no real opportunity for a private conversation. Gabriel had networked furiously and she was beginning to see why he was such a success at work. The couple sitting on the other side of him were looking for new legal representation and by the end of the final course he had them well and truly in the palm of his hand. She couldn't fail to be impressed. His work was a world away from hers.

Eventually there were just four people left at their table. Another couple on the opposite side were talking quietly and Gabriel turned to Lucy. She picked up her water glass to keep her hand steady, and took a few sips. The champagne had made her feel light-headed and the last thing she wanted was to get drunk.

'You haven't asked me once about Ed,' she said. Talking about Ed would keep her mind where it ought to be.

'I know,' he said. 'But when we last discussed Ed you asked me to stop meddling. I thought I'd overstepped the mark a bit on that one.' He took a sip from his own glass and looked at her over the rim. 'Still going ahead with the proposal, then?' He raised a questioning eyebrow.

She looked at him. 'I know we argued before I left the flat, but it was my fault really. Everyone argues sometimes in a normal healthy relationship.'

He nodded, non-committally.

His silence made her feel compelled to press on. 'Ed is feeling a bit unsettled with me at the moment. I don't think he's sure of where he stands any more.' She looked at Gabriel and shrugged. 'I can't really blame him, can I? Suddenly I start dressing differently. I start hanging out with you more. He thinks there's something going on between us.' She let out a little laugh.

'Would that be so funny?' Gabriel asked. He was smiling, too, but his gaze was very intense. She felt unable to tear her eyes away from his.

'No…yes…of course not.' She struggled to say what she meant without offending him or giving her feelings away. 'I just meant it was a mad conclusion to jump to, that's all. Mad for you and me, I mean. To him it seems a logical explanation.'

Gabriel looked at her a moment longer, then shifted his gaze over her shoulder towards the band, who were preparing to raise the noise level of the mellow background music they'd played during dinner.

Lucy took a deep breath and tried to direct the conversation at Gabriel, to take the spotlight away from her. She hadn't talked to him about relationships since the night she'd mentioned Alison. 'Did you think any more about settling down yourself, Gabe?' she asked. 'Looking for Miss Right? You can't carry on for ever, you know, the eternal bachelor. One day you'll meet the right person. Settle down, have kids…'

A shadow crossed his face and he still didn't look at her, watching the band playing behind her. 'Maybe I already have met her,' he said, eventually. Then he stood up purposefully. 'Come on. You can't come to a ball and not dance.' He held out his hand.

'You know I can't dance, Gabriel,' she protested. 'Two left feet, that's me.'

'Rubbish! Just hang on and follow me. No one here really knows what they're doing anyway.'

After a moment she smiled and gave in. It was dark after all. She'd had a few drinks and the band were playing 'Moon River'. The perfect tempo for someone like her. All you needed to do was sway a bit and you were there. She took his hand and let him lead her as he picked their way through the couples on the floor. She caught her breath as he slid one arm firmly around her waist and entwined her hand in his.

She picked the conversation back up where they'd left it. After the night when they'd looked after Steven, she knew now he wouldn't bite her head off if she mentioned his past. 'You can't carry on letting what happened with Alison affect you for the rest of your days,

Gabe.' He was holding her hand tightly but she still managed to free a finger and point it at him. 'I should know that better than anyone after the last week or so. Who'd have thought I could see a future with my parents back in it? I know it's hard but sometimes you have to let go of the past and move on. For years I thought I had moved on but it turned out I was dragging all that baggage along with me. Ignoring it instead of really sorting it out. I'm actually lighter now. I really am.'

For a moment Gabriel said nothing, and without talk to distract her she became acutely aware of how close he was to her. She could feel the hard muscles of his thighs, strong from all that rugby in his youth and from the gym now, hard against her own through the thin silk of the dress. He let go of her hand and moved it around her to join the other one, pulling her even tighter to him. She rested her hand against his chest, acutely aware of the breadth of his shoulders, the strength of his arms encircling her. His breath was warm against her hair as he spoke.

'When I said I'd already met her, I wasn't talking about Alison,' he said.

He pulled back from her far enough so he

could look clearly and deliberately into her face. The words, the way he'd spoken them, full of meaning, resonated in her mind. She felt as if the moment lasted minutes, not seconds. Every nerve ending in her body was totally aware and fine tuned. Every touch of his body against hers sent dizzying sparks to her stomach, her heart, her mind. The touch of his fingers lightly stroked her bare spine, the other hand folded tightly around her waist so as to hold her close against him. His aftershave, woody and spicy, filled her senses and she felt literally weak at the knees, as if she might suddenly fold into a puddle on the floor.

'Gabe…' she tried to say. She wasn't sure herself what words she would follow his name with. His name filled her mind leaving no room for anything else. He leaned slowly forward and his mouth perfectly caught the curve of hers. His grip tightened on her as if he wanted never to let her go. The music filled the room but the band could have been playing anything or nothing at all. She took none of it in. There was nothing but the feel, the smell, the touch, the taste of him. There could have been a million people in the room, but for her there was no one else but them. Nothing else but this kiss.

As they broke gently apart he didn't speak or even look at her, he simply held her close against him and continued to move gently. For Lucy it was as if the music had suddenly been turned back up. With a jolt she became aware of the room again, the people, the sounds. And her mind suddenly had room for everything else. What the hell was she doing? How could she have allowed this to happen? Where was her resolve? She felt a wave of sudden anguished guilt. Ed had been right to be suspicious of her. Poor Ed, how could she behave so badly towards him? The man she was supposed to love. And Gabriel. Their friendship. What damage had they gone and done? The thought smashed into her mind, chasing out all the warmth, all the delight from moments before. She pushed Gabriel away from her, eyes wide, rubbing her hand across her mouth as she did so, as if she could erase what had just happened, go back to the way they were before.

She saw his eyes widen, a worried expression surfacing, but she wouldn't allow herself to stay and see more.

'Gabe, I'm sorry, this isn't right. I…I have

to go,' she said finally and turned before she could give him any chance to speak. Whatever he had to say she didn't want to hear. The damage they had just done to their friendship. How could she have let it get this far? She must have been giving him unconscious signals. What would he expect now—a three-week fling? She wasn't about to waste the last twenty-three years on that. There was only one thing to do to try and save the situation and that was get some serious distance between them. Right now. She ran from the ballroom, down the stairs and into the darkness, leaving Gabriel standing alone in the middle of the dance floor.

CHAPTER EIGHT

GABRIEL stood outside the hotel and pushed an exasperated hand through his hair. Where the hell had Lucy gone? He looked left and right but the road in both directions was empty except for parked cars vaguely visible in the streetlights. She must have found a taxi from somewhere. It was beginning to rain but he was oblivious to it as it soaked his hair and dampened his designer suit. What the hell had he gone and done now?

He hadn't meant to kiss her; he truly hadn't. From the moment she'd stepped out of her front door earlier he'd had to keep himself on constant guard to hide his attraction and he'd been doing a pretty good job, if he said so himself. It was the dancing. He should never have asked her to dance but he hadn't liked the way the conversation was going and it had been all he could think of to do to divert her and stop her talking. He'd known the instant her body was against his that he had no hope left. He rubbed his fingers slowly across his lips as if he could still taste her on them. The softness of her skin under his hands and the delicious scent of her hair had removed all the control he'd had in place. The thin fabric of her dress had meant he could feel every contour of her body against his. The kiss had been the most natural, most right and perfect moment of intimacy he could ever remember having. And now he'd screwed it up.

He turned and walked back into the ballroom to make his excuses and leave, walking the perimeter of the room to try and avoid one of his ex-girlfriends, who was making a beeline for him. He needed desperately to think. One thing was certain though. The way he felt right now he wasn't going to let her go. Not without a fight.

Lucy let herself into her flat with shaking fingers. Her curls were damp and beginning to frizz from the rain. For one awful moment she wondered if Ed would be there waiting for her but the place was quiet and in darkness. She heaved a sigh of relief.

She was shaking all over. The combination of the freezing weather and the after effects of that kiss. She'd never felt such an acute physical response to anyone before. She'd been powerless to stop it. She was staggered by just how right it had felt. Especially when her head had been—and still was—telling her constantly that the whole thing was totally wrong.

She turned on the light in the sitting room, kicked off her high heels and went to slump on the couch. And it was then that she saw it. A piece of paper left on the coffee table.

'Sorry. Call me,' she read, in Ed's scrawling handwriting. Her eyes filled with tears that quickly blurred the words. What had she done?

Gabriel tried for what felt like the hundredth time to call her but the landline at the flat simply rang endlessly and he assumed she must have unplugged it. He'd been pressing redial since he'd walked back through his front door. Her mobile phone informed him that it was switched off and suggested he try later. It was no good, and he had no idea why he had expected anything else. Why would she react differently to this than she did to every other difficult issue or encounter in her life? He'd known her since she was six and her policy in all that time had been the same. Disengage from the rest of the world until you've worked out what to do. Except he was very worried that if he didn't get to talk to her soon her choice of what to do might not include him at all. He picked the phone back up. He'd just have to keep on trying.

Lucy stood under a steaming shower, letting the water pour down over her closed eyes. She struggled to understand what the kiss really meant to her. *He feels the same way as you do,* her mind whispered. And if that was true, it put things in a whole new light. Should she just brush it off as one of those things, a slip-up? Did Gabriel want her as more than a friend? And if he did what did that mean? A short-term fling before he backed off just as he always did? Their friendship might be able to survive a slip-up of a kiss but it could never survive more than that.

Then there was Ed to think of. Her heart twisted when she thought how hurt he would be if he knew what she'd done. She'd been so happy with him for a long time. She had such plans for them. How could she ever make him understand or forgive her? And even if she could, what hope of a future was left for them now? Crushing her feelings for Gabriel felt like an impossible task; even shoving him out of her mind for a few minutes wasn't achievable at the moment. Her guilt was growing; she felt she was adding to her betrayal just by thinking about him.

She climbed into bed. It was late and she was tired out from the stress of the evening. But sleep was a long time coming. She finally fell into a thin doze at about three and was awake again by six. Throwing on some old jeans and a T-shirt, she went straight to the kitchen and began lining up sugar, eggs and flour on the worktop next to the mixing bowl. She needed to think things through.

Gabriel was up early on a Sunday for the second time in a month. *And both times it's been Lucy's fault,* he thought wryly. He couldn't let things lie. Not the way he felt now, and not the way he'd felt last night. It had gone too far. He climbed into his car and started the engine. Whether she was ready or not, they needed to talk.

* * *

Lucy made sponge cake mixture on autopilot. She was barely aware of what she was doing, but as usual with her hands busy she was able to think clearly. Guilt gnawed away deep in her gut. It was all Gabriel's fault. She'd had everything under control and he had to ruin it. She passed a flour-covered hand over her eyes. *Don't lie to yourself, Lucy.* There was nothing to be gained in trying to make herself feel better about what she'd done. *The only person to blame for all this is you. You could have pushed Gabriel away, laughed it off. Instead you played as much of a part as he did.* More, in fact, because Gabriel was a free agent and she was supposedly on the brink of marriage.

She tried to think clearly, work out how she felt. She took the two ends of the spectrum in turn. Ed. Reliable, kind, loving. Clumsy but endearing. Ambitious in his own haphazard way. She'd always know where she was with Ed; he was predictable, and that made him safe. And to someone with a background like hers those things were to be prized, treasured.

Gabriel on the other hand. Incurably, undeniably ambitious. He'd clawed his way up in legal circles. Partner of the leading firm of solicitors in Bath. Now courting senior partnership and still not even thirty-five. Interesting that he'd rejected London after his initial training contract, wanting to work his way to the top of a smaller firm where he could have some major influence from very early on. He thrived on the buck stopping with him. Inescapably unreliable. Fickle, commitment phobic. Best friend anyone could ever want. Better brother than a real one could be. Sparky, inspiring, challenging. She never felt as if she would win hands down with Gabe, whereas with Ed she was always firmly in the driving seat.

She wondered how Gabriel was feeling, what he wanted from her. For all she knew he could be filled with regret right now. Maybe he'd drunk too much champagne and was now cursing the demon drink for getting him into this mess. While she tortured herself about her behaviour he could be embarrassed and wondering how to let her down gently. Her instinct was to call him, find out what he wanted from her, but guilt wouldn't let her do that. Infidelity had played its part in the demise of her parents' happiness and in her eyes it was symptomatic of a ruined relationship. It hurt to think of herself and Ed like that. Whatever Ed's faults were, he didn't deserve to be treated so shabbily. And she felt so low about herself. She who prided herself on her total control of her life and her destiny, acting on impulse like that. She shook her head. She simply didn't *do* impulsive; she did rational.

She knew one thing. She couldn't have Gabriel near her until she'd sorted this out. It was all she could manage right now to stop thinking about him, about how he felt and tasted. To speak to him or meet him would qualify as infidelity in her eyes now, after what had happened between them, and she wouldn't do it. She owed it to Ed to sort things out with him before she did anything else. That could be the only way she had of feeling good about herself again.

She reached across the counter and turned on her mobile. The second it found the network there came beep after beep of text alerts. Just as there always was when she and Gabriel argued. He never could let it lie. She knew him well enough to be certain that before long he would give up on the telephone and come to find her in person. She couldn't have that. She would have to call him and tell him to give her some space. But before she could decide whether to read his texts or go straight to the point and ring him, the phone itself broke suddenly into Elvis singing 'Blue Suede Shoes'. Ed must have reprogrammed her ringtone again. An incoming call. She glanced at it and her pulse increased and not in a pleasant way. Caller ID showed her that it was Ed on the line. She felt absurdly exposed, as if by her picking the call up Ed would by some sixth sense be able to tell that she'd kissed Gabriel. That she'd betrayed him.

She pulled herself together. She just needed to get this conversation out of the way and then she could get her head straight and work out how to make things right. She picked up the phone.

'Ed, hi!' she cried, in an overly bright tone of voice, which belied the guilt that stuck like a bone in her throat.

'Lucy.' He sounded a little confused. 'I wasn't sure you'd pick up after last night.'

Her heart pounded. What did he mean 'last night'? Had he somehow heard what had happened?

'I'm really sorry for everything I said,' he went on, and she suddenly realised he'd just meant that he was expecting a frosty reception. After all, the last time they'd spoken had involved her slamming the door on him and then swiftly leaving in Gabe's car. Any lingering irritation she might have felt about yesterday's argument had since been beaten into submission by her new guilty role in the situation. But Ed didn't know that, of course, and she needed to inject some normality pretty quickly if she was going to avoid him guessing something was up. She wanted to talk to him calmly about this once she'd had time to think it through, not blurt it out over the telephone and end up with another flaming row.

She covered her eyes with one hand. 'Ed, it's fine. Really it is. It was my fault, not yours. I was so preoccupied with getting ready to go out that I never thought how it might make you feel.'

'Don't say anything else. I saw you looking so beautiful and I got jealous. That was all. Jealous that you'd be spending the evening with Gabriel and not with me. I had no right to shout at you. I know Gabriel is just a friend, I should never have implied anything else.'

Her face burned with shame at this. How was she ever meant to make this right?

'How was the night out, anyway? Did Gabriel make senior partner?' He sounded genuinely interested, eager to hear all about her evening and make up for the things he'd said.

'It was rubbish,' she said quickly. 'Boring group of dull career-obsessives.' She tried unsuccessfully to push the image of Gabriel's kiss out of her mind.

He sounded mildly surprised. 'Shame. I know you were looking forward to it. Well, maybe I can make up for it tonight. And it'll give me a chance to say sorry properly for yelling at you.'

She couldn't bear this. Couldn't bear him being so apologetic when she'd betrayed his trust without a second's hesitation. Her eyes filled with tears and she swallowed hard.

'Ed, please. I've told you there's nothing to make up for.' Her discomfort came out in her voice as irritation and it only made him even more persistent.

'There is. I insist.'

She clutched at her hair in frustration. *Stop apologising!*

'Come to The Abbey with me tonight,' he coaxed. 'Have a fun time, talk things through, eh?' The Abbey was the bar they visited most often together.

She leapt on this. Talking properly was exactly what they needed to do. Not some stilted excuse for a heart-to-heart over the phone. She knew she had to tell Ed what had happened. She had known since she'd left the party. The kiss weighed on her conscience like a stone. She could spend today thinking how best to handle it, find some way to try and make things right. And perhaps being on neutral ground instead of in her flat or his place would help.

'OK, that would be good,' she said. 'Can I meet you there, say seven-thirty? I need to drop some things off at the shop on the way and I'll come straight there.'

'Great!' The delight and relief in his voice compounded her sense of discomfort even further. She couldn't bear being in the same room as herself right now. Her mind refused to quit the endless reruns of Gabriel's kiss, which seemed to make her heart race even harder every time she relived it. She had to get things straight. Now she just needed to keep Gabriel away until she'd seen Ed and her mind was clear. As Ed cut the call off she took a deep breath and clicked speed dial for Gabriel.

She didn't get far. As she waited for the line to connect the entry buzzer sounded suddenly in the hall, making her jump. She walked down the hallway as if in a dream, her hands covered in flour, and picked up the intercom.

Gabriel stood outside on the step. His heart pounded as he waited for her to speak.

'Yes?'

'It's me,' he said simply. There was no need to say any more.

Her voice was laced with panic and he longed to give her a cuddle and tell her everything would be fine. 'I can't do this right now, Gabriel. I need to sort things out with Ed.'

'Just ten minutes. Please. You know we need to talk.'

'I need you to stay away from me…'

He couldn't believe what he was hearing. Sort things out with Ed? He had to get her to talk to him, let her know how he felt before she stormed ahead with the proposal to Ed on some guilty impulse.

'What? Don't be so ridiculous. You can't pretend nothing has happened, Lucy.'

'I'm not pretending!' Her voice took on an angry tone. 'But until I've seen Ed, talked things through, seeing you will just be cheating on him. Even more than I already have. And I won't do that. I won't make things worse than they already are.'

He didn't like the way she was heading with this. The only way to deal with her obstinacy sometimes was just to storm on regardless and so he tried again.

'Lucy, please. I need to talk to you. Ten minutes, that's all.'

'What part of no do you not understand? Please, Gabriel, just go away.'

'I'm going to say what I've come to say, whether you like it or not, Lu. So you can either let me in or the whole street can hear me yell it through the intercom. It's up to you!' He raised his voice to emphasise his point.

A long pause. And then she pressed the entry button.

Lucy opened the flat door and went back to the kitchen without waiting for him to come up the stairs. Her heart was thundering in her chest and she hoped that concentrating on the cake she was making would keep her calm. She heard the door slam as he came into the flat and she turned as he entered the kitchen.

She could see by his face that he'd probably had even less sleep than she had. There were dark smudges underneath the grey eyes.

'I wish you'd turn your phone on now and then,' he grumbled. 'I've spent the last six hours trying to call you.'

She glanced across at the phone on the kitchen window sill. 'I know. I only turned it on ten minutes ago and it practically rang itself off the shelf with all your texts. One message would have been enough, you know.' She picked up a wooden spoon and began beating the cake batter although it was all perfectly mixed already. At least it meant she didn't have to look into his eyes and hold that grey gaze. Her stomach did cartwheels every time she did that. It seemed her body knew perfectly well what it wanted. To be carried by Gabe down the hall and straight into her bedroom. But she had to control her body with her mind, and that was telling her to be careful. Be very, very careful. She needed to follow her head, not her heart. She'd built her whole life around doing exactly that. *Don't throw away twenty-three years plus a future with Ed, if you can somehow salvage one, on something that will last five minutes, Lucy.*

Suddenly he was standing very close behind her and she felt weak. If he tried to kiss her now she wasn't sure she had the presence of mind to stop things and talk to him. But he simply reached around her and took away the bowl of cake batter. Hands left with nothing to do, she turned around and leaned back against the counter, folding her arms across her body.

'We need to talk, Lu,' he said simply.

She looked up at him. His eyes held hers. 'I know,' she said.

'I'm really sorry about last night,' he began.

Her heart began to sink, telling her how deep her feelings for him went. It made her feel guiltier than ever. Did he mean it was a mistake? That he regretted it? If so, how should she feel about that?

Anxious not to give away her own feelings—that would make her vulnerable—she gave a neutral answer. 'So am I.'

His face fell a little. 'I'm not sure you understand, Lu. I'm not sorry for kissing you. I'm really not. I'm sorry because I haven't been honest with you and you deserve a lot better than that.'

She rubbed a hand tiredly across her forehead. 'What do you mean you haven't been honest?' she asked him.

'I don't want you to propose to Ed.' She stared at him. The words spun in her mind. 'You're not still thinking about it, are you?' He searched her face.

'To be honest I don't know what to think.' She took a deep breath and looked down at her hands. 'Up until last night it was all clear to me and now I feel like I don't know where I am. It's all your fault. None of this would have happened if you hadn't kissed me.'

Gabriel raised his eyebrows at her sharp tone. 'Quit kidding yourself, Lu. You're just trying to pass the buck because you feel guilty about Ed. I can understand that. I can. I feel bad about Ed, too, but that doesn't change the facts. I might have been the one who started it but you didn't exactly fight me off, did you?'

She felt a hot blush of shame rise in her face. He was right. It made it feel momentarily better if they both shared the blame, but that was just window dressing. She had to take responsibility for her own actions, not dilute the repercussions by using Gabriel. It annoyed her that he knew her well enough to read her mind.

He grabbed her hand, entwining his fingers

in hers. 'That kiss meant as much to you as it did to me. Don't deny it, Lucy. Not to me.'

She made the mistake of looking into his eyes and she felt light-headed. She would not let herself lose control again. A repeat of last night was *not* going to happen. Not while Ed was in the picture. She couldn't erase the kiss they'd shared but she could damn well stop things going any further. With a stupendous effort she removed her hand from his grasp and stepped away, putting cooling space between them.

She had to keep a handle on the facts here or she would go under. She felt awful for discussing anything with him before she'd been able to see Ed. Just talking about the possibility of being with him felt like cheating. But the fact was that she needed proper commitment from Gabriel if they were ever to go anywhere. Proper certainty that what had happened between them was different from his usual relationships. She needed to know he was ready to commit again, not get cold feet after a couple of weeks. This had to come from him. He was the one who was incapable of taking a relationship seriously, of giving it his all. If all he was after was a fling then she would stop the whole thing now, however hard that might be. She forced herself to ask the question that frightened her the most. 'What do you want from me, Gabriel?'

He moved towards her again, reclaiming the space she'd put between them, and took her hands in both of his. His huge hands enveloped her small ones easily, her fingers tingling at his touch. Her heart was beating so hard she thought he might be able to hear it.

He looked seriously down into her eyes. 'I want you, Lucy. I want you to drop the proposal with Ed and give things a try with me instead.' He smiled at her, his eyes crinkling at the edges, the lopsided smile she loved so much lighting up his tired face.

She didn't smile. 'What do you mean by "give things a try"?'

'Try being together as a couple. Not just as friends. For starters we could have a proper night out, just the two of us. Nothing heavy, just a relaxing evening. And then I thought we could both do with a break, so maybe we could think about taking a couple of weeks off, going somewhere hot. What do you think?' He looked at her expectantly. He thought she would jump at the chance, didn't he? Why wouldn't he think that? she supposed. Every other woman did.

Her heart was deflating. She could almost feel it in her chest. Disappointment flooded her. He hadn't changed at all, had he? She remembered some of those lines, almost word for word, from the night he'd met Ed's friends and flirted with Joanna. And why on earth did he think a holiday in the sun was the way to go? As if a relationship between them wasn't unreal enough, he was suggesting they take it and put it in an artificial setting with perfect surroundings. When they came home she knew the honeymoon would be over. And so would their friendship. What she needed to hear was that he was prepared to throw one hundred and ten percent into it alongside their everyday lives and challenges. She took her hands away from his and walked into the sitting room.

'What's wrong?' He followed her, sounding genuinely confused. 'What did I say?'

She sat down on the sofa, elbows on knees, and blew a stray tendril of hair out of her eyes. She looked up at him and shrugged. 'It's more what you didn't say, to be honest, Gabe,' she said.

He frowned. 'I've laid my cards on the table,

Lucy. This whole proposal thing of yours, spending time with you, looking at you gaining confidence, sorting things out with your dad. I realised the last thing in the world I want to do is help you get married to someone else. I tried not to show it, God knows I did, but last night it just got the better of me. And there's no point me trying to hide it any more. I've fallen for you and I want you to be with me.'

'Gabriel, our friendship means everything to me.' She looked up at him. He was standing with his arms folded indignantly. Still frowning. *He's not used to women knocking him back,* she thought. *I do believe he thought he'd come here and I'd just fall into his arms.* 'So much that I'm just not willing to risk it by having a fling with you.'

'Hang on a minute—'

She held up a hand. 'Let me finish.' She was firm but quiet. For once she had her temper under total control.

He looked at her impatiently. 'OK, go on.'

'Last night, Gabe, when you kissed me.' She dropped her eyes shyly and looked down at her hands. 'No one's ever made me feel like that before.'

He was across the room in three quick

strides, kneeling in front of her, his hands on hers again. 'Then let's give it a go,' he said softly, his mouth so close to hers that she could just touch it in a slight movement, take him down the hall to bed right now. 'What have we got to lose?'

She pulled her hands away and forced herself to stand up. 'Everything, Gabriel. And that's exactly the problem. I don't want to lose you as a friend and if we go ahead with this and it doesn't work out I'm scared that's exactly what will happen. Your relationships last five minutes. And then you can't turn back the clock. Things would never be the same. We'd have lost everything. So if this is just about you panicking because I'm settling down, there's no need. Nothing will change for you and me, Gabe. We'll always be best friends, no matter what.'

He stood up next to her and looked intently into her face. 'It's not about that. It's about us being more than just friends. I've changed, Lucy. I can make this work. And I promise you that, no matter what happens between us, we will always be friends. Always. You don't need to worry about ruining that by being with me.'

Could she really believe that? She looked

at him and swallowed hard to keep the threat of tears at bay. She wouldn't let him see her cry; she was absolutely determined about that.

'I need time to think, Gabe. I feel terrible for just talking about this with you while Ed's in the dark about what's happened. I can't think about anything until I've sorted things out with Ed. I have to make things right with him—you must see that. I can't just pretend last night never happened. I'm not the kind of person who can gloss over that and then sleep soundly at night. All this is too sudden. I need to work out what I'm going to do.'

'Well, you can't still be intending to propose to him,' Gabriel said boldly. 'Not now.'

Her temper stirred. 'Why not?' she asked. 'Because you say so?'

'Because of what happened. The way you just said you feel. You can't go ahead with it now.'

'Maybe I can't. But even if things finish with Ed it doesn't automatically follow that diving into a relationship with you is the right move. Try and see it from my point of view, will you? You're suggesting I throw away a good relationship, one that was good enough, by the way, for me to be ready to marry the guy, for you, who has the track record of a rock star for making relationships work. Already you're suggesting we go away on holiday. What I need is to know we could work in the real world before I would ever take a chance on it working out in some unreal holiday environment.' She sighed. 'You mean the world to me, Gabriel, as a friend. I just don't know if I can give that up. How do I know you've really changed? That you're really ready for this—a proper, grown-up, serious relationship?'

This was getting her nowhere. The way things were headed they would end up having a row. She needed to clear her head, decide what to do. 'I need you to leave, Gabe. I'll call you later.'

His face fell. 'No. I'm not leaving. We need to talk this through.' He grabbed one of her hands. 'Please, Lucy.'

'I need to think!' she shouted at him. 'Stop pushing me, Gabriel!' And then her voice broke a little as she lowered it and tried to speak calmly, to make him listen. 'I need you to get out now and give me some space.'

He dropped her hand as if it were suddenly red hot. 'OK, OK.' He held his hands up submissively. 'I'll go now. Give you time to think.

But listen…' He moved back towards her a little, as if he couldn't stop himself, and clenched his fists. 'Just promise me you'll think about how it could be between us,' he said. 'We have so much going for us—you can't deny that.'

She only gazed back at him steadily until he left the room and she heard the front door bang shut behind him. He hadn't once mentioned proper long-term plans. Something in Gabriel had been broken all those years ago when Alison died. Could she really believe that one kiss with her had mended it? That he now had the capacity to give her everything she needed? Because she needed security and safety to be happy, she needed to rely on him in the same way she needed air.

Gabriel didn't bother going home again after he left. He felt that the prospect of their relationship was balanced on a knife edge. He felt uneasy. Had he really given it everything he'd got? Had he really opened his heart to her and let her see in? Or had a decade of keeping women at a distance, avoiding any danger of loss, made him hold back? He didn't know. But if he'd got this wrong he would lose her anyway now and he wasn't sure he could stand that. He knew her well enough not to paint her into a corner, knowing that would only make her dig her heels in against him. The only thing to do was to back off and give her time to think. And it had to be her choice at the end of the day. What she wanted. Not something she'd been pushed into, but something she embraced.

He turned the car in the opposite direction to his flat and made for the motorway. For Gloucestershire. He was determined to get this right. Lucy would never settle for anything less than marriage; he knew that. If he had any chance of winning her over he had to be prepared to be with her for always, to put aside all his fears that the past might repeat itself and that he might lose her the way he'd lost Alison. He had to take a leap of faith. He found with surprise that the idea filled him with nothing but hope and delight. He had spent years avoiding even the thought of it. He just hoped that when she was ready to talk, he could make her listen.

Lucy opened the oven and removed the mess inside. She'd put the cakes in before Gabriel arrived and had forgotten about them. They were burnt and rock hard. A total disaster. She hoped that wasn't a reflection on her life. She felt emotionally drained and exhausted. She did her best to try and think clearly but her mind felt groggy and slow. What she needed was fresh air and she longed for a run by the river to clear her mind. She wasn't sure of what she wanted to do, of where to go from here. So Gabriel didn't want her to propose to Ed. But he didn't seem sure how he wanted things to proceed between them. He seemed afraid to commit to anything more than 'giving it a try'. Was she not worth more than that? Surely gambling their friendship meant more to him than that.

She had no idea whether she and Ed could work things out, but, even if he could forgive her behaviour, would it be right for her to stay with him after this? Could she live with the lack of passion that came so easily to her with Gabriel as long as she had the settled security that Ed had always given her and that was so important to her?

Or did she risk everything, literally everything, on Gabriel? Her stable relationship with Ed, her friendship with Gabriel, which was more like a family tie really, her home because if something went wrong with Gabriel she couldn't live here, not any more. Heart or head? Which way should she jump? When it came right down to it she was scared. Scared of everything she had to lose.

Gabriel sat in silence in his house. He was deep in thought. Ed's message on his answering machine had been blinking away when he'd got back from the swift visit he'd made to his family home. Still unable to shake the sense of unease that had descended on him when Lucy hadn't simply fallen instantly into his arms, he was immediately put on edge at the sound of Ed's voice. Had Lucy spoken to him? Already? He began to frown as he listened to the short message.

'Er, right…Gabriel?' A pause. 'Not there, then?' Gabriel raised exasperated eyes skyward. For all his business aspirations Ed had yet to master the art of the slick answering machine message.

'Ed here. Lucy's Ed.'

The way Ed spoke, as if he somehow belonged to Lucy, made Gabriel bridle with jealousy. He might not hold Ed in particularly high regard but there was no getting away from how much Ed had meant to Lucy for a considerable time. He would be a fool to underestimate that.

'Just wondering if you can make it to The Abbey tonight. Half-seven-ish. Bit of an evening planned and I'm sure Lucy would like you to be there. Bye, then.'

The machine clicked off. What the hell did this mean? She couldn't have told Ed about them, then, as she'd said she was going to. Was she having second thoughts? Or was this some kind of ruse on Ed's part to get him in the same room, have it out with him? Gabriel had no feelings of guilt. In his opinion Ed didn't deserve Lucy; it was as simple as that. If he'd been up to the challenge she would never have been tempted to look at anyone else. It was Ed's own fault if she found what she needed elsewhere. He knew in his bones that he, Gabriel, was what she needed—it was just convincing her of that fact that was the problem. Lucy felt guilty enough for the both of them, it seemed.

He picked up the square velvet box that rested on the table in front of him. It opened with an almost inaudible squeak. Nestled inside was an ornate emerald ring in a Victorian setting. He took it out and twisted it between his finger and thumb, studying it. The green was the colour of Lucy's eyes. It had been his grandmother's. After Lucy's reaction today he had known he had to find a way to convince her that he could offer the lifelong security and love she craved. Maybe this ring, a piece of his family, to which she'd always dreamed of belonging when she was a child, could help him do that. He snapped the box shut. Whatever this evening was, whatever happened, he intended to be there. He intended to fight for her now in any way he could.

The Abbey was a popular bar showing a mixture of live music and televised sport. Somewhere in the course of her relationship with Ed it had come to belong to them in the way bars and pubs sometimes did when you visited them often enough. As she walked down the steps and through the door into the mellow darkness, dotted with flickering hurricane lamps on tables, Lucy's stomach was a knot of nerves. Perhaps by the end of the evening she would have some clarity about her feelings. About what she wanted to do.

She needed to talk things through with Ed. If everything had been right with their relationship she would never have looked to Gabriel for more than friendship. Yet the moment she had begun to think about pushing for commitment from Ed, her long-buried feelings for Gabe had begun to resurface. Slowly at first but gathering momentum until at the dance she had been unable to exert the self control she always believed she had when it came to principles like infidelity. The physical and emotional way Gabe touched her transcended all rational thought.

She was clear about one thing. She had to be totally honest with Ed about what she had done, how she had let him down. She wasn't sure Ed would still want to talk to her, or even look at her after that. She couldn't let herself think about Gabriel until she'd gone through with this.

She glanced automatically towards the table halfway down the room. Years of sitting at it had given it the tag 'our table' whenever they attended together and both of them felt irrationally aggrieved if anyone else dared to sit at it. She stopped and stared. There was no sign of Ed but Yabba, Suzy and Kate were sitting there, drinks in hand. Digger was standing at the bar and raised a hand in her direction as he caught sight of her. And was that Joanna sitting with her back to the door?

She felt a surge of exasperation. So much for an evening of in-depth soul-searching with Ed. After their argument he'd obviously decided that the perfect way to get things back on track was a night out with all their friends. As if on cue she noticed Ed himself striding across the room from the stage area where the live music, a jaunty-looking man with a synthesizer and backing track, was setting up. So not only an evening with their friends but an evening of shouting all conversation over blaring music. She tried not to tense up as Ed swept her into a hug.

'Great, you made it! Come on, let's get you a drink.' He pulled her by the hand towards the bar as the jaunty man kicked off with a loud sixties track. Ed raised his voice to compensate. 'Orange juice?' he shouted.

She nodded. 'Ed.' She tugged at his sleeve to get his attention. 'Ed!'

He looked round.

'I thought we were going to talk,' she half yelled. 'You know. After yesterday. Straighten some things out.' She could see Digger standing behind Ed, very deliberately not listening, and she frowned at him. He looked away.

'We will, we will! No harm in having a good evening out though, eh?'

He gave her waist a squeeze and she felt an odd sense of unease at his enthusiastic manner. Ed was behaving weirdly. She wondered for a moment if she'd got it wrong on the phone and if he really had somehow found out about her kiss with Gabriel. Was he going to make some kind of scene? She dismissed the thought immediately. Ed was a straight-down-the-line kind of guy. He didn't have hidden agendas; they weren't his style. She was just on edge because of the weight of her conscience. And the way the evening was going there was no way she'd be able to do anything about that here.

They made their way to the table and she reluctantly took the vacant seat between Ed and Joanna.

'How's Gabriel?' Joanna asked her at the first opportunity.

Oh, for heaven's sake. 'He's well, as far as I know,' she said shortly. How could she be expected to put Gabriel out of her mind when people kept mentioning him at every turn?

'Ask him yourself, Jo,' Ed said, raising a

hand in greeting towards the door. He kept his other arm clamped firmly around Lucy's shoulders in a gesture of possessiveness that didn't escape her notice.

Lucy's heart felt as if it had been jump-started; she felt her pulse begin to race. Not a gradual climb in heart rate but an uncontrollable leap. She turned to look. The bar might as well have been empty. For her there was no one else here. The irritating music faded to a background hum. Her green eyes met his grey ones and she was home.

Why didn't Ed make her feel like this? Not just now, but ever. She couldn't remember a time when she'd looked at Ed and thought that the world could end right there and then and she wouldn't give a damn as long as she was with him. Gabriel crossed the room and sat down opposite her. Every cell in her body was in a heightened sense of awareness. Her desire for him was so acute that she worried the others would guess her innermost thoughts, and she tried hard to avoid looking at him.

As Ed kissed her cheek and stood up to speak to someone her rational mind kicked in with another twist of unease. What was Gabe doing here? This wasn't one of his haunts; he preferred the trendier wine bars and night-clubs closer to the city centre. She felt a sudden prickling of worry that maybe he intended to confront Ed with what had happened between them, force the issue despite all they'd said that afternoon. She couldn't do that to Ed. For heaven's sake, all she wanted was the chance to come clean to Ed, to treat him with the decency he deserved, and yet all people and circumstances seemed to be thwarting that.

As soon as Joanna had finished her effusive greeting of Gabe—did she need to kiss him on *both* cheeks?—Lucy leaned in across the table towards him, fighting the urge to reach out and touch him.

'What the hell are you doing here?' she asked in an awkward stage whisper, trying not to draw attention from the others. Especially Joanna, who looked none too pleased at having Gabriel diverted.

'Ed invited me.'

Her heart felt like a brick in her chest. 'Why would he do that? He never calls you up, invites you anywhere. He leaves all that to me, if we ever see you socially. Which we hardly ever do.' She looked at him urgently. 'What is going on?'

'Well, I did wonder, to be honest. I actually thought you might have told him about us. I was almost ready for a showdown even though he said you'd be here, too.'

'Of course I haven't told him. I can hardly talk things through with him in front of this lot, can I? Not that I can hear myself think anyway!' She sat back in her seat and cast a nasty look at the entertainer, who was continuing with his hideous set of sixties and seventies music, singing along to an awful backing track. Just at that moment Yabba brayed a loud guffaw two seats away from her that wouldn't have sounded amiss on a donkey. The place was bedlam. And then the last straw: the music suddenly changed to the booming introduction of an Elvis Presley number.

'Oh, you can't be serious! This bar has the worst live music in Bath!' she shouted. She grabbed her orange juice angrily. Nothing was going to be resolved tonight and she might as well get used to it.

'Is that Ed?' Joanna said suddenly to no one in particular.

The hand clutching her orange juice froze en route to her lips. The table fell gradually still as one face after another turned towards the stage. Lucy followed Gabriel's shocked gaze to the pool of light in which Ed stood, holding a microphone attached to a stand. Her eyes took in every detail against her will in glorious sharp colour. Ed was wearing a silver jumpsuit—*a jumpsuit!*—encrusted with coloured plastic gemstones that caught the light. Even as she watched he struck a pose, opened his mouth and burst into a heavily exaggerated Elvis impression. Her lips pulled back from her teeth in an uncomprehending grimace. An enormous Elvis quiff perched on top of his head. He had even blackened his blond sideburns to match the awful wig. Her eyes refused to leave out the slightest grisly detail as he threw himself with gusto into murdering 'The Wonder Of You'.

Gabriel was motionless opposite her, an expression of dumbstruck amazement on his face.

'I didn't know Ed could sing,' Joanna said.

Ed's voice built to a warbling crescendo, his authentically trembling lip visible even from across the room. He seemed to be working on the policy that loudness would counteract lack of tune. As Lucy watched him through stunned eyes he struck another pose to end the first verse, one hand plastered to a jewel-encrusted hip, the other stabbing the air above his head with a pointed finger.

'Well, let's be honest about it. He can't sing, can he?' Yabba said as Ed's voice took on a screechy pitch.

Mercifully one verse seemed to be enough for him. It was certainly enough for everyone else as a stunned silence fell for an excruciating moment before scattered clapping kicked in. Lucy was transfixed as Ed took the microphone from the stand and began to make his way across the room towards her. The spotlight followed him. He spoke into the mike as he walked.

'That was for mah Lucy.'

She realised with horror that he was staying in character.

'I love ya, little lady.'

'I had no idea you were an Elvis fan, Lucy,' Joanna leaned in and said to her as Ed progressed between the tables, the spotlight taking in his every move.

'I'm not,' Lucy heard herself say. Her mind and eyes didn't seem to be engaged with each other properly. Was that really Ed? What the hell was he doing? 'Not really. Ed's a massive fan, though. Always trying to indoctrinate me…'

Her voice trailed into nothing as Ed finally reached her table. Beads of sweat hung on his face. Was he really wearing fake tan? She was vaguely aware that the spotlight was taking her in, too, now and she knew just from the way her face burned that she was a bright tomato red.

She had no time to think, no time to collect herself. Whatever she'd been expecting from the evening it certainly hadn't been this. It was like some surreal dream and she half expected to wake up and find herself in bed at home.

Ed flung himself theatrically onto his knees at her feet. Looking up at her and still in character, he crooned in a deep-voiced southern drawl, 'Will ya marry me, baby?'

Opposite them, in the darkness outside the spotlight, Gabriel was choking on his drink. Joanna stood up and thumped him artlessly on the back. Lucy didn't notice. Too late, the penny had finally dropped. Silence fell around her. She was suddenly unaware of anything except for the stares of everyone in the room boring into her, taking in the pair of them bathed in the light. Ed gazed up at her, a silly grin plastered across his orange tinted face, an expectant look in his eyes. And before she knew what she was saying, before she even knew what she was thinking, panic and confusion spoke for her and the word was out of her mouth.

'Yes.'

The room exploded in wild applause, whistling and cheering. And she was swept suddenly out of her seat and into Ed's arms. He twirled her around, her feet inches from the floor, in a bear hug. As their friends crowded around them, slapping Ed on the back and kissing Lucy's cheeks, the music relaunched into an horrific funked-up version of the 'Bridal Chorus'. Like a rush of ice water through her veins the realisation of what she had just done swept through her and in alarm she looked around wildly for Gabriel. She was too late. The door swung shut behind him and all that was left was his half-empty drink on the table.

CHAPTER NINE

GABRIEL glanced around the hallway of his house. Somehow he'd managed to get himself home on autopilot. He remembered none of the physical journey from The Abbey whatsoever. Every ounce of his energy had been spent turning what had happened over and over again in his mind. And in trying to stem the sensation that his heart had somehow been crushed, stamped on and kicked into pulp.

He couldn't believe she'd said yes. Not when she'd spoken the word and not now. And without wavering, without hesitation or even a glance in his direction. Weren't women in two minds supposed to go for the neutral answer and say they'd think about it? That was what happened in the movies and he couldn't for the life of him fathom why it hadn't happened tonight. If she'd had anywhere near the feelings for him that he'd thought she had, then, surely yes would have been the last thing she'd say.

He could kick himself now. Her ridiculous proposal idea. He'd contributed to this. Lining up Amanda to give her a makeover, making Ed sit up and take notice. In a surge of desolation he remembered that a couple of weeks ago this had been her dream. Ed proposing to her. The end of her rainbow. Was it such a leap that when her dream came true she would grasp it with both hands? It seemed entirely possible right now that the kiss, everything they shared, might cease to mean anything to Lucy in the face of the future with Ed that she'd so desperately wanted before.

Lucy watched Ed soaking up the attention from friends and strangers alike in the bar. She needed to get him out of here, somewhere quiet where they could talk. Less than a month ago this would have brought her ecstatic happiness. Ed proposing. The beginning of having a proper family of her own at last. How ironic. *That stupid proposal plan, Lucy. Be careful what you wish for.*

She was horrified that she'd agreed to marry Ed. How could she have done that? She'd just gone and made things a million times worse. Yet even if she hadn't panicked, how could she possibly have done anything else? After the flamboyant way he'd proposed could she really have crushed him in front of all their friends? She couldn't help remembering Gabriel's advice to her back at Smith's. It seemed like months ago now but it was only a matter of days. He'd told her not to propose in front of their friends if she didn't want to force a false 'yes'. And he'd been right. If you cared about someone you couldn't humiliate them like that, so you would take the only other option. Say yes at the time and then do your best to undo it later. That was what she'd have to do now, if she could ever disentangle him from his adoring public.

Two hours were long gone before she managed to get him back to her flat. Even then she'd practically had to manhandle him into the Mini. Now he threw himself back onto Lucy's sofa and sprawled there, letting out a noisy sigh. He was still wearing the silver Elvis jumpsuit, had insisted on wearing it for the rest of the evening as their friends applauded his performance and congratulated them both. He had dispensed, though, with the ill-fitting wig, and his fake tan paled to white at his hairline, the blond hair changing to black at the sides of his face. Lucy had eventually managed to persuade him to leave the party and come back to her flat, and now he leaned back comfortably, arms spread wide, grinning at her sitting-room ceiling.

'What a great night, eh, babe? You know, Suzy said we should go to Graceland as part of our honeymoon. Not such a bad idea, is it? Could do the whole tour. Visit the King's grave, everything. What do you think?'

There was silence for a long moment before she finally took the plunge and spoke.

'It's no good, Ed.'

He looked up in surprise at her quiet tone, such a marked contrast to his overexcitement. He saw her looking at him seriously, steadily. He sat up properly.

'What do you mean?'

She took a deep breath. 'It isn't going to work, Ed.'

His eyes widened.

'I really wish it could work. But I've been deceiving us both. And I've been totally, unforgivably unfair to you.'

Her eyes filled with tears at the expression

on his face. This was not some easily disposable two-date boyfriend. She had loved Ed. She had. The fact that it had been more with her head than her heart didn't demean him one bit. She blinked hard. She had to get this over with. He deserved someone who loved him with passion, not someone who was just making do.

As he came back into focus she could see in his face that he'd guessed what she meant. But she needed to voice it anyway, say it out loud.

'Ed, when I went to the dance with Gabriel…' she began. She had to try and find a way to explain, to somehow make things between them not *right,* exactly, she could never do that, but at least make them better.

He interrupted her unexpectedly. 'You know, Lucy, tonight was a spur-of-the-moment thing really,' he said. 'After that row we had I tried to come up with something that might cheer you up. But now that it's over with and I've had time to think, well…'

She watched him, waiting for him to carry on.

He was looking at her, his eyes not wavering from hers, his face contemptuous. She wanted to look away from the onslaught of his hurt reaction, ashamed of how she'd made him feel, but she made herself meet his gaze. He deserved to say his piece.

'You know I've always tried to be what you wanted me to be. You've always harped on about marriage and kids but you know I've never really been the marrying kind. Then after that row the other night I thought if it was what you wanted I'd go through with it to keep you happy, that's all.' He made a disgusted face. 'I was wasting my time, wasn't I? What I really think now is that we should scrap the whole thing. And not just the wedding plans. Everything. I should have listened to my instincts the other night about you and Gabriel. I think I knew, even then. You're not what I want or need any more. Maybe we've had our time, run our course.'

'Ed…' She shook her head at him.

'It's OK, Lucy.' He smiled at her. A strong smile. No cracks in his voice. 'We've had some fun, haven't we? Don't be sad. You'll soon get over me.' He grabbed his jacket in one swift movement and turned for the door.

She jolted out of her stupor as he reached the hallway and crossed the room to swing around the corner after him. He was standing at the end of the hall, the door of her flat held open.

'Ed!' she cried in an anguished tone.

He turned back.

'Ed, I'm sorry.' Her voice cracked. She looked at him, trying to show in her face how true that statement really was. That she regretted her treatment of him with her heart and soul.

He smiled at her. Dignified resignation showed in his face. There was no attempt to talk her round. She didn't blame him for that; it was no more than she deserved. She'd betrayed his trust. 'Goodbye, Lucy,' he said. The door clicked shut behind him.

She stood and looked at the closed door for a few minutes, gathering her thoughts. In a way that door had shut on everything she'd taken for granted. The easy option where she'd always have been able to predict life at every turn. As she calmed down she felt no regret, no pang for that mapped-out life. She walked slowly back into the sitting room and automatically checked her phone for texts from Gabriel. She found herself looking at the screen in dismal surprise. Nothing. No calls. No messages. For the first time ever he appeared to be able to cope with them being at odds with each other. Didn't he care? She tried to ignore the sudden fear that this was a knockback too far for Gabriel. An accepted proposal in front of all those people. Maybe he was washing his hands of her.

She refused to believe that. She put the phone down on the table and dismissed the impulse to dash to his house and explain. Instead she would let the dust settle. There was something vaguely disrespectful to Ed in rushing to Gabriel the instant the door had closed behind him. Plus the fact it was late now. Past midnight. She would wait until the morning before doing anything. And, she told herself, Gabriel would have definitely got in touch by then anyway. He couldn't stand tension between them for long.

Gabriel Blake gave up trying to sleep a little after three in the morning. He made his way to the kitchen and brewed coffee he didn't really want, just for something to do that wasn't lying down thinking about her. He wondered how long it would be before he could sleep soundly again and didn't hold out much hope.

His initial shock at Lucy's acceptance had

given way now to a gnawing sense of loss. The thought of her planning her wedding in delight, marrying Ed, making a home and then down the line starting a family filled him with utter desolation. How could he bear to watch that? To see her, a happily married woman, all the time wishing she belonged to him. Torturing himself over the question whether he could have done something, anything, differently. Perhaps if he'd been clearer, stronger with her when he'd told her how he felt. He passed a weary hand over his eyes. It was too late for that now. He'd missed his chance.

He realised with a rising sense of despair that he'd lost her. It was a different kind of grief from the way he'd felt when Alison had died but that didn't diminish the magnitude of it. He had lost her not just as a lover, a wife, but also as his best friend. Because he couldn't see a role in her life for him that wouldn't amount to daily agony as he watched her loving someone else.

Lucy woke up early, the shock of everything that had happened blasting into her mind like a hammer blow. She grabbed her mobile from the bedside table. It hadn't disturbed her sleep even though she'd left it switched on and she could immediately see why. No texts. No missed calls. No communication from Gabriel at all. She couldn't believe it. It was so unlike him and the implication that he no longer cared what she did brought tears springing to her eyes. She rubbed them away angrily with the back of her hand.

She needed to talk to him, to explain. *What if he doesn't want to hear it?* She refused to accept that possibility. Scrolling through her phone list, she called Sophie to tell her she'd be in late and arranged for her to open up the shop. Then, heart thumping in her chest, she dialled Gabriel's number. It took ages for him to pick up. It was so unlike him. She was used to him hounding her after they argued, or when one of them did something to offend the other. It had always infuriated her, but she would take it a million times now over this desolate silence from him. Maybe he'd decided to cut her from his life completely. Decided that she wasn't worth the effort or the grief. Her heart twisted agonisingly at the thought.

Just as she thought he was going to carry on ignoring her—she had no idea how she would deal with that—he finally picked up.

'Lucy.' How tired he sounded. It pulled at her heart.

'Will you meet me?' she asked him. 'Can we talk?'

There was a long pause. She bit her lip.

'Is there really anything to say, Lu? I'm happy for you. You've got what you wanted, what you planned for, haven't you? I know you're worried about us staying friends but I think maybe it's best if you just get on with things for a while. I'll keep a low profile for a bit.'

Her eyes filled with tears. 'Gabriel, please. I haven't. Got what I wanted, I mean.' She clutched at her hair in frustration. 'This is such a mess! Will you please just meet me? Just for ten minutes? After that I'll leave you alone if you want me to, I promise.'

Silence fell again, but her determination was kicking back in. After all this time, all this anguish, she wasn't going to be put off this easily. If he wouldn't meet her she'd damn well just go round to his house and ring the doorbell until he let her in. If he didn't want anything to do with her he could tell her to her face, after she'd told him how she felt. At least then she'd know she could do nothing more.

A sigh. 'Where?'

She clenched her fist in triumph. 'Pulteney Bridge. Half an hour.'

He hung up without saying goodbye.

Gabriel put the phone down. Hope tried to infiltrate his desperate heart, but he was too quick for it. He'd thought he'd all but won her last time they'd spoken and then last night had happened. He knew how much their friendship meant to her. And that she must be terrified of losing it. He wished he could tell her what she wanted to hear, that he'd be there for her for the rest of her life, just as he always had been, but he couldn't watch her make a family, grow old with someone else, all the time wishing it were him.

He loved her. When it came right down to it, he loved her. And he couldn't bring himself to refuse to meet her. But he intended to keep it short and make it clear that he needed space. Just how long he would need it for he wasn't sure. A lifetime? He didn't know.

He grabbed his car keys and prepared to leave the house. And then at the last moment he turned back from the door. Before he could stop himself he picked up the ring, still in its box on the counter, ready to be returned to his parents the next time he visited, and pocketed it. He knew he was tempting fate but he didn't care. If he sensed the slightest possibility of convincing her to go back on her marriage plans, he intended to fight for it with every ounce of strength in his body.

CHAPTER TEN

LUCY waited patiently by Pulteney Bridge. She wasn't expecting Gabriel to be on time—why would he break the habit of a lifetime? She looked over the stone railings down at the river. The rush of water on the weir below was soothing.

'Lucy.'

She turned from the water to face him. Who had she ever been trying to kid? All those years since she'd buried her feelings for him when she met Alison. All those years had led up to this moment. She was here with the hope of spending all the days of her life after this one with him. She might have been able to convince herself once that there could be another option. That she could squash her feelings and just keep his friendship. But not any more. The thought of giving him up now caused her such acute pain that it felt physical, not just emotional. As if her body and soul would be crushed alongside one another if she had to forgo him now. Had he felt so let down by seeing her accept Ed's proposal that he'd decided it wasn't worth the risk? No, she couldn't let herself think that way. She had to make him understand.

Two weeks ago and her suggestion that they meet at the bridge would be undisputed shorthand for only one thing: a joint run. Things were different now. Nothing was assumed in their relationship any more. The easiness between them was gone. At the very least they couldn't pick up their friendship where they had left off.

They moved away together from the huge stone railing and she followed him down the steps to the path that ran alongside the river. Her heart pounded in her chest the way it did when she'd gone for a run, as she had done with Gabe so many times down this very path. Just walking next to him, knowing he was close enough to touch her, made her limbs feel like jelly, her skin tingle deliciously.

She looked up at him just as he glanced down at her. Nerves writhed in her belly as if she were on a first date. She was determined to go through with this, no matter what happened. He might reject her out of hand, but if she didn't try she'd never know. Her lifelong craving for security wasn't enough on its own. She couldn't base her life, her relationships, on that need alone. Not now she knew the depth of passion she was capable of feeling.

'How's Ed?' he asked. A heavily loaded question.

She looked down at the path. He believed them to be together of course. But why wouldn't he? He'd witnessed firsthand her unwavering acceptance of Ed's outlandish proposal. In her panic she hadn't even hesitated, had she? The question that bothered her now was how he felt as a result of it. He didn't exactly look as if he was burning with jealousy—not such a good sign.

'He's fine,' she said. 'As far as I know.'

She picked up instantly on his slight change of posture. A sudden sharpening of his attention. He stopped walking and touched her arm. Not a strong hold, just a tap to get her to look at him.

She did. She took in the thick dark hair, the determined set of his strong jaw. The grey eyes, which looked almost blue today in the sunshine that was taking the edge off the cold air. She could see he looked tired and before she could stop herself she raised a hand to touch his face. He immediately covered it with his own and electric shocks crackled in her fingers, her stomach, her thighs.

'As far as you know?' He searched her eyes.

She gazed steadily back at him. 'Ed and I are over, Gabe.'

'But last night…'

'I should never have said yes. You know that, don't you? You were there. You saw the trouble he'd gone to. He thought he was losing me to you and so he decided to stake his claim.' She sighed. 'Making him jealous, changing my clothes. My stupid proposal plan. All of that worked in the end. How could I humiliate him in front of all his friends by saying no? You told me yourself proposing in front of all our friends would be a mistake.'

She searched his face for some reaction but he looked completely neutral, unreadable. 'I talked to him afterwards, came clean about what went on between you and me. I wish I'd been upfront with him before I'd let things get that far between us, but I honestly thought I was in control.' She sighed. 'It's no excuse. But I've done the best I can to put it right.'

'So what do you want to do now?' His expression was cautious, giving little away. Of course he was cautious. She'd told him before that just because it wasn't right with Ed didn't automatically make it right with him. He had listened to her. He was letting her have total control this time.

She looked down at her feet. 'I know things have been complicated since the dance, and I'm sorry about that, Gabe. You have to know that I had no choice but to sort things out with Ed before I could talk to you. Ed's proposal just made things even more difficult. But the thing is…' she glanced up at him shyly '…when I realised I'd rather have a three-week fling with you than a lifetime with Ed, there was no contest really.'

An amused expression appeared on his face and he took her hand in his. 'In what universe do you think three weeks with you would ever be enough?' he asked her gently. 'I'm not even sure a lifetime would be enough for me. I know my track record is rubbish, I know you probably think the odds of me holding down something long term are minuscule, but, Lucy, I can promise you that's what I want. To be with you, build a future. You have to believe me.'

Her stomach was doing flip flops. She tried to keep her voice steady. 'I'm really glad to hear you say that,' she said, allowing herself a nervous smile. 'Because although I mentioned the three-week-fling option, it was never really going to be up for grabs. You know me too well for that. Our friendship means far too much to throw it away for a fling. And anyway, I always aim high.'

Her heart began thumping as she took a small step backwards from him and dropped to one knee on the cold paving. The river flowed by behind him, the sun bouncing off its surface. She looked up at his face. An expression of surprise and sudden understanding rose in his eyes.

'Gabriel,' she said, and his name caught in a snag of emotion in her throat. So much depended on this moment. He could still say no. She cleared her throat with a croaking sound. Oh, great. Just what was needed for the perfect proposal: a Kermit the Frog impression.

'Gabriel,' she tried again. 'Will you mmmmf—?'

He was on his knees next to her, grey eyes

level with her own, his hand plastered firmly over her mouth stopping the words mid-sentence. She frowned and grabbed his big hand with both of her small ones, tugging at it until he let her pull it away.

'What are you doing?' she asked in a panic. He was stopping her before she could make a fool of herself. He was letting her down gently. Despite what he'd just said, marriage wasn't what he wanted, then. Would she sacrifice her marriage dream as long as she had him? Her heart tightened a little. Of course she would. In a second. How much she had changed.

He smiled at her. 'It's not February twenty-ninth any more, Lu. We're into March now, in case you didn't notice.'

Was that it? The nervous energy she'd expended on this and he was quibbling about the *date!* She pointed an indignant finger into his face, just inches from her own. 'I've loved you since I was sixteen years old, Gabriel Blake. That's my entire adult life. And I am *not...*' she raised her voice an insistent notch '...waiting another four years just so I can ask you on the correct day!'

His eyes crinkled in amusement as his face broke into the lopsided smile she loved.

'So this is your last chance,' she said. 'Don't blow it.' She took a deep breath. 'Gabriel, will you mmmmmf!'

His hand was back against her lips again. She could smell the faintest trace of his after-shave, spicy and deep, making her stomach feel soft. She was glad she was on her knees already as she wasn't sure they would have held her up much longer.

He smiled as she wrenched at his hand again. And then her eyes widened and she quit tugging instantly as his free hand produced something from his back pocket. A tiny velvet box.

'No, Lucy,' he said. 'Will you?'

At last he took his hand away so he could flip open the box for her. But even with her mouth free, she couldn't find any words. She gazed down at the most exquisite emerald ring she'd ever seen. It sparkled up at her.

'It was my grandmother's,' he said, as if he couldn't bear the silent wait for her answer. 'I thought you'd like it better than something I picked up in a shop.'

'It's beautiful,' she whispered. His face was inches from her own. Warmth began to sweep slowly, deliciously through her. He'd put aside his commitment fears. Made the biggest gesture he possibly could to prove it. For her.

'Of course I'll marry you.'

She was in his arms. She was spinning, light-headed, as his mouth crushed hers and his fingers tangled in her hair. She could feel the muscles of his shoulders beneath her hands and she felt his heart hammering like a drum against her own. She was acutely aware of his hands beginning to wander lower, snaking down her back, and she thought she might actually faint onto the cold paving.

The sudden rush of a bicycle flying past them, almost close enough to knock the pair of them into the river, brought them both back to reality with a jolt and Gabriel helped her to her feet, laughing. They linked hands and walked slowly back up the river path towards the city centre.

'You'd better not backtrack on that acceptance tomorrow,' he teased her, sliding an arm around her.

She elbowed him in the ribs. 'Very funny. You didn't ask me in public, did you? So yes means yes—you needn't worry.'

He gave her waist a squeeze. She was acutely aware of his arm circling her, of his touch. The thought of being alone with him made her quake with anticipation.

'Where to, then—home?' he asked her.

'Where is home exactly? Don't you mean "your place or mine"?'

'No, I mean home.' He squeezed her fingers. 'I want this to be proper, from the outset. And much as I know you love that titchy flat, Lucy, you have to agree my place is bigger and we need the space for all those endless bits and pieces you buy from tat shops.' She made as if to slap him, and he dodged her, laughing.

'Anyway, you rent, I own. Move back in with me. You know you want to.'

Her flat held no strong ties for her now. She realised she associated it very strongly with the past and Ed. Perhaps it would be a good thing to let it go. And it demonstrated again how serious he was about them being together. There was no hedging his bets this time with suggestions of holidays.

She grinned at him. 'Only if you promise to relinquish the remote control once in a while and make sure you put kitchen equipment away in its designated drawer.'

'Agreed,' he said.

They continued for a moment in silence. A

comfortable silence. His fingers knitted loosely in hers. Her stomach was a mass of soft knots.

'Do you think I should have asked your dad's permission?' he asked her suddenly.

'Are you joking?' She looked up at him with an incredulous expression. 'We might be back in touch but the only person who makes decisions about *my* life is me.'

'With reference to me? And maybe our kids one day?'

She smiled up at him. 'Deal.'

* * * * *